Norma Jean and the Mystery of the Gypsy Summer

N.J. Bennett

Norma Jean and the Mystery of the Gypsy Summer

Norma Jean Mystery Series

Written by
Norma Jean Bennett

Illustrated by
Bronwyn Bennett Lane
WynnsicalWorks

Produced by
Megan Bennett

Bennett Hall Projects

Copyright © 2014
Revised © 2018
All Rights Reserved

ISBN 978-1494467975

**The Norma Jean Mystery Series
By N.J. Bennett**

*The Mystery of the Suitcase in the Ditch
The Mystery of the Gypsy Summer
The Mystery of the Midnight Tea Party*

Norma Jean's Notebook

Storyboarding with Norma Jean

Look for the <u>Norma Jean Mystery Series</u> on Amazon
or at **bennett-projects.com**.
Follow us on Facebook and Instagram!

Lovingly dedicated to my Mum and Dad,
Florence and Andy Nielsen, who knew how to
provide creative space for their seven
children. Ya done good, 'rents.

And again, many, many thanks to my two
daughters, Meg Bennett and Wynn Bennett
Lane and my man, Roy, who just plain love
me and support my many crazy ideas.

Table of Contents

Chapter 1
A CAJUN BOY *FANTASTIQUE*

Gyp was talking in his sleep. Norma Jean could see the moonlit silhouette of his supine body. She sat up in her bed, pulled the Hudson Bay wool blanket up under her chin, and stared at him from across the cabin. The wood coals still flickered hot in the cast iron stove and eerie shadows tumbled haphazardly around the room.

"But I don't HAVE the key," Gyp moaned. "I NEVER had it. I don't know WHO has it..."

Norma Jean looked over at Howard, who was sleeping soundly in the bed beside her. *Useless.* She looked at Gyp one more time, then lay down and went back to sleep.

***

It smells so good in here—and it's warm.

Norma Jean rolled over, pulling her blankets over her ears. With an effort of the will she tried to push morning away and pull her dream back.

"Coffee's ready!"

Norma Jean opened one eye. *Shoot*. Morning pushed back at her and her dream got away. She'd have to search for the key some other night.

"Coffee's ready, Norma Jean. Come on, get out of bed."

The early morning summer sun slid around the face of the cabin and peeked through the screen door. Norma Jean opened both eyes. Howard's gaping mouth, in the bed next to hers, interrupted her gaze. She blinked as he let out a loud snore.

"Hey, Howie! The day's half over. Get out of bed for the love of St. Afan!"

For the love of St. Afan? Making a final effort to dust off her sleep, Norma Jean propped herself up on one elbow.

"Do you take it black?"

She sat up. There, in the middle of the cabin, a muscular, dark-haired boy of 12 was using a long willow stick to rearrange the fire in the belly of a wood stove.

"Coffee?" His dark, piercing eyes smiled at her.

She pulled her flannel sheet up to her chin. "I'm only 12. I don't drink coffee and neither should you. And Howard doesn't drink coffee either. He's only 11."

"Wow. You've got a lot to say for an early morning." He grabbed a blue rag from the line that was strung from one side of the cabin to the other.

Wrapping it around the handle of the coffee percolator, he poured the dark, syrupy liquid into a tin mug.

"Here," he walked over to her bed and handed her the mug, handle towards her. "Go ahead, take it."

Making sure the top button of her pajamas was fastened, she reached out and took the mug. Looking at him over the rim, she said, "There's oil floating on top of this coffee."

"Course there is. You know what they say about coffee." He poured himself a cup, winking at her as he did so.

"No. I don't." Norma Jean raised a wary eyebrow as she watched him.

"Coffee should be 'sweet as love, black as night, and hot as hell.'"

Norma Jean's eyes widened as she sat there on the bed, coffee in hand, staring at him. Finally she said, "Says who?"

"Old Arab proverb."

"My hair's a problem! We're at the lake for pity sakes," Howard threw his arm across the bed.

Gyp laughed. "I said, *old Arab proverb,* not *your hair's a problem.*"

Howard blinked, then grunted as he rolled over.

"Wake up Howard," Norma Jean said, "Coffee's ready, and we don't care what your cowlick does for the rest of the summer." She took a sip of coffee as the boy watched her. "And the coffee's great!" she smiled.

Howard wiped the drool off his cheek and threw his red wool blanket to the end of the bed. "Lots of sugar, please," he said, rubbing his eyes.

"Right you are." The boy poured another cup of coffee and handed it to Howard. "There you go, Howie. Sugar's on the table."

Norma Jean watched as Howard got out of bed, light-green pajama pants falling slightly low, and his brown shirtless tummy rumbling for breakfast. He took a giant step toward the table and put six sugar cubes into his mug.

"We've never called him Howie before," she said.

"Norma Jean," Howard stirred his coffee. "I'm right here. You sound like you're talking about a dog. *Howie*. I like it. You can call me Howie." He took his coffee back to his bed, sat down and leaned against the wall.

"Speaking of dogs. Where's Nicky?" Norma Jean held out her cup as the boy topped it off.

"No doubt gone to see that mutt down at the campground's store," Howard said.

"Mutt? If you're talking about that Catahoula Leopard, that ain't no mutt. That's a coondog. I saw him this morning before Nicky—if that's your black lab—ran off with him. Yup, that there is a regular coondog. Never thought to see one in these parts."
Norma Jean and Howard stared at him, then Howard took a sip of coffee, "Phew! That's...that's..."

"With six sugar cubes, it oughta be 'sweet as love.'" The boy laughed again.

"What?" Howard looked at him.

"Never mind." Gyp winked at Norma Jean. He climbed onto the end of her bed and sat there, cross-legged. "Do you mind?"

"N-noo." She looked at her brother nervously. "Come on Howard. There's room for you too."

He moved one bed over and they sat there sipping coffee—all three of them, cross-legged on the bed, looking at each other.

"So, is Gyp your real name?" Howard asked the boy.

"Nah. It's short for Gypsy."

Norma Jean looked at him. There was something wild about this boy. His light complexion complemented his black, straight hair. She could see why he was named Gypsy.

"Ya mean your name is Gypsy?" Howard crinkled his nose as he took another sip.

"Just a nickname." He turned his attention to Norma Jean. She checked the top button of her pajamas again. "I think I fell asleep in the middle of your story last night, Norma Jean. I'd been traveling all day. Tell me again about this place."

Norma Jean looked around the spacious one room cabin. "Well, it's been in the family for ages. I think it belonged to Mum's great-grandfather or someone. This whole property did—15 acres right here beside Pine Lake."

"Hey, wait a minute," Howard interrupted. "Before you start talking, I'm hungry. Let's go up to the big cabin and eat. Mum's probably got breakfast ready."

"I asked your Mum if I could make us breakfast here."

Norma Jean stared at Gyp. "When? When did you ask her?"

"This morning, sleepyhead." He held his coffee steady and rolled his body off the edge of the bed. "She gave me sausages and eggs."

"And coffee?" Norma Jean asked.

"Well, no, I brought that with me." Norma Jean looked at Howard. He raised his eyebrows and shrugged.

"Keep talking while I make breakfast, Norma Jean."

He placed a cast iron pan on the stove and moments later threw some pork sausages into it. They sizzled immediately as he shook the pan from side to side.

"Well," Norma Jean continued, "we come here every summer and stay—in-between planting and harvest time. It's only eight miles from our farm..."

"Will I get to see your farm?" Gyp gave the sausages another shake.

"Oh yeah. We go back all the time to look after the garden..."

"And get more food," Howard interrupted.

"Dad and the boys..."

"The boys?"

"Our older three brothers: Allan, Les, and Keith. They go to work there everyday."

"Doing what?"

"Getting the swather and the combine ready for harvest and all that stuff."

"The wha...?" Gyp interrupted his own interruption. "Never mind. You can tell me about that later. Tell me about the cabins."

"This one is the old one; I guess that's obvious. Howard and I have cleaned it up so we can live in it during the summer. It has everything we need: stove, table, chairs, beds, shelves. We've even got a few old books for a rainy day." She pointed to the plank that had been nailed at eye-level beside the closet, on which were about a dozen musty old volumes. "You found the pump, I see, with our excellent well-water..."

"Excellent?" Howard scoffed. "Yes," he mocked, "We have EXCELLENT well-water..."

"Oh be quiet, Howard," Norma Jean laughed, just a little embarrassed that he should make fun of her in front of Gyp.

Gyp laughed too. "And EXCELLENT well-water is what's needed for STUNNINGLY good coffee."

Howard groaned.

"EXACTLY right." Norma Jean raised her nose at Howard and joined the laughter. *Okay, maybe it's going to be all right...*

"Keep talking, Norma Jean," Gyp said.

"Oh, I can't believe you just said that," Howard banged his head several times on the wall behind him.

She ignored him and said to Gyp, "You must have gone inside the big cabin to get this basket of food. Did you? Was there anyone there besides Mum?"

"Yes," Gyp replied, "Your mom... I like how you say *MUUUM* by the way." He exaggerated the *U*.

Howard and Norma Jean looked at him and then at each other. Howard shrugged his shoulders.

Gyp continued, "Your mom was there, and baby Barry...but I met them both last night. Your sister, Kathy, is actually the one who put the basket of food together for me."

"Of course she did," Norma Jean rolled her eyes.

"She's really nice," Gyp said.

"We know," Norma Jean said. "Anyway, about these cabins..."

Norma Jean looked out the screen door toward the sprawling cabin that was a stone's throw across the hay field from them. It was about the same size as a barn and looked very much like one, expect the *loft* wasn't there, only a normal house roof. It was painted red and the roof was covered in dark green shingles.

The big cabin had one small bedroom partitioned into the south-west corner. Mum and Dad slept there and they all used it as a changing room. The rest of the floor plan was open. At the same end as the bedroom was a simple kitchen, boasting a very large wood stove, an equally large kitchen table, and some cupboards. The rest of the family slept on any one of the dozen or so chesterfields that were haphazardly arranged around the big room. It was, as Mum liked to say, *rustic*. And that's just how everyone liked it.

She did a little verbal tour for Gyp and assured him that they would show him everything in time.

"Dad built the big cabin before Howard and I were even born and even though there's lots of room there for everyone, Howard and I always stay here. We like it best."

"I can see why. It's *fantastique*!" Gyp rolled the sausages to one side of the pan and began cracking eggs into it. He shook the pan again while grease and smoke flew into the morning sun rays. Norma Jean and Howard looked at each other, and Norma Jean, again, raised her eyebrows.

"I'll set the table." Howard jumped off the bed.

"Wait a minute," Norma Jean interrupted. That table cloth needs to be shaken out. Last night's crumbs are all over it. She picked up the daisy patterned cotton cloth, folded it and took it out to the porch. There, she shook it out, vigorously. *Much better.* She brought it back in, and arranged it on the battered and scarred oak table. Howard placed three blue-green melmac plates and three knives and forks on the freshly shaken cloth.

"Done! Let's eat." He arranged three mis-matched wooden chairs, one in front of each place.

Gyp wrapped the rag around the pan handle and brought breakfast to the table. "Here we are. Breakfast fit for a band of Cajun Gypsies." He dished it up, put the pan out on the porch to cool and sat down at the table. "Dig in."

Howard looked at Norma Jean then said, "Don't you pray?"

"Holy St. Afan! Of course I pray." He bowed his head while Howard and Norma Jean listened, wide-eyed.

"Dear God. If Holy St. Afan is up there with you, and I expect he is 'cause his tombstone says *Saint*, tell him I'm doing just fine. I'm still writing his prayers since he didn't have time to do it before he died. And here's one of them:

O Thou who dids't create all the food in the whole world; we thank thee especially for pigs and chickens. Now please, bless our sausage and eggs. Amen."

Norma Jean and Howard sat there for a moment, hands still folded on the table. "Boy, that was different," Howard finally said, "but I expect it worked. Let's eat."

Gyp filled his coffee cup. "Hope you don't mind that I'm staying here with you." He looked at Howard and Norma Jean. "I mean this is your cabin after all."

"Are you kiddin'? We love it!" Howard forked a sausage and began eating one end of it. "Especially if you can cook."

"Norma Jean?" Gyp's dark eyes held her own and Norma Jean felt her forehead bead ever so slightly.

"It's fine," she croaked. It had been much easier to talk last night. He had been lying in the bed on the other side of the room and she didn't have to see him. Clearing her throat, she tried again. "Ya see that closet there?" She pointed with her fork to a gray, pink and green patterned curtain. "It's really big and has a window inside of it. Howard and I take turns changing in there. As you can see this cabin is just one big room..."

"Got it," Gyp said. His voice trailed off and he took a sip of coffee.

Norma Jean waited for a moment, then continued, "Lucky for you there's three beds here. You can have that one by the door for the whole summer." She motioned with her head to the bed he had slept in last night. The table separated his bed from the other two, and the stove was against the wall at one end of the table. A big metal pipe went from the stove through the roof. "I'm sure you found the outhouse in the willow trees behind us."

"Yup."

"There's no electricity in this cabin. Howard and I like it that way. At night we light the Coleman lantern. Last night we just used flashlights because we got home from the airport so late. Dad had already made the fire for us but Howard and I usually do it ourselves."

"The coals were still hot this morning. I'll have to thank your dad," Gyp said.

They ate in companionable silence. When Howard finally pushed his chair away from the table, Gyp said, "So, where's the lake?" He picked up their dirty plates and carried them out the screen door to a large table set against the wall of the porch. It was covered in a yellow oil-cloth, with red roses on it. The eastern morning sun shone through the pines that guarded the front of the cabin.

"Ah, that sun is inviting us to come join the day. '*You are my sunshine...*'" He began to sing as he pumped water into the tin basin and washed the dishes. The porch was screened in above a three foot wooden wall that encompassed it. A dilapidated roof covered it all. The screen was in very poor repair and the four wide steps were rickety and worn. Dad, however, had done an inspection and declared that the cabin was *safe* for Norma Jean and Howard's summer usage.

Norma Jean and Howard followed Gyp out of the cabin, sat on the porch steps and watched him. "In front of the big cabin there's a trail that goes through the trees, down the hill, to the lake. We made the trail ourselves. And the beach too. In fact, Dad and the boys did everything here except build this cabin," Norma Jean explained. "As I said, this cabin's been here for ages."

"Jumping St. Afan! This is going to be a great summer." Gyp stacked the plates, put his hands on his hips and did a jig. Howard and Norma Jean just stared at him.

Finally Howard said, "Who's St. Afan?"

"What? You don't know who St. Afan is? Welsh Saint of course. All they know of him is a tombstone that proved he lived. That's why I help him with his prayers." He looked at them. "Of course, since we're Cajun I SHOULD be celebrating Mary, as SHE is our patron saint," he crossed himself, "but I like Saint Afan, and since he died before he wrote any prayers, I think he must be grateful to me..."

Norma Jean and Howard gaped at him.

Gyp laughed, "Sorry. I'm a bit of a talker. Just tell me to stop when you can't take any more."

"Talk all you want. We don't care." Howard lay back on the warm porch steps and sighed. "I like the way you say your words. It's kinda different."

"We ARE related ya know," Gyp continued.

"I guess we do, now. Know it, I mean," Norma Jean said. "We don't really know much about it though because Dad and Bedstefar and Bedstemor are so...so...Danish."

"Who?" Gyp interrupted.

"Our Danish grandparents," Norma Jean said. "We didn't even know Mum had any relatives from...what is it? Louis...?"

"Louisiana," Gyp drawled. "And here I am in the flesh." Gyp sat down beside them. He was already dressed in khaki shorts—the kind with lots of pockets —and a bright orange T- shirt. "*Laissez les bons temps rouler!*" he shouted.

Norma Jean looked at him from the corner of her eye. *Who in the world is this kid?*

"What?" Howard asked.

"Let the good times roll!" Gyp laughed. "It's gonna be a *bon* summer."

Suddenly remembering she was still in her pajamas, Norma Jean jumped up from the porch. "I'm going to get dressed." Holding the top of her orange and green polka-dot pajamas closed she grabbed her clothes and disappeared into the small curtained closet.

"I'm changing in here. Nobody come in." She waited, listening for some response. "I said, no one come in!" Pausing for another second she heard Gyp murmur something and Howard snort coffee through his nose as he started to laugh.

Stupid boys.

She pulled on last winter's Levis that were now this summer's shorts and added a white T-shirt that read, Seattle's World Fair. It had belonged to one of the boys and Norma Jean liked how soft it had become with age. She grabbed her socks and runners and went back to sit on the porch. Howard had changed into cut- offs and a black T-shirt with a green John Deere tractor on it. Norma Jean sat down beside him as they both tied their runners. They could see Gyp walking through the cabin's overgrown yard, stopping every once in a while to examine a plant.

"What do you think?" Norma Jean whispered to Howard.

"'Bout what?"

"Gyp, you idiot."

"I like 'im."

Norma Jean pulled a hair elastic out of her pocket and tied her barely shoulder length blonde hair into a ponytail.

"Didya like that coffee?" Howard grinned.

"Uh-huh."

"Let's go show Gyp the lake." Howard jumped off the steps and jogged toward Gyp.

"I'll meet you there!" she called as they turned to wait for her.

Norma Jean watched the boys run off toward the big cabin. She walked down the steps and turned right, toward the outhouse. There was a hedge of wild roses behind it and she wanted to gather some to put in that mayonnaise jar she had found on the cabin shelf. As soon as she got there she realized she'd forgotten a knife to cut the sturdy stems. She turned abruptly around and felt the swish of a blackbird as it flew too close to her and landed on the outhouse roof .

"Bug off, you stupid thing," Norma Jean said, as she picked up a small rock and hurled it toward the blackbird. "You scared the crap outta me...and I'm no CANDYASS!" She looked around, making sure no one heard her say that word.

After arranging a big jar of roses on the inside table, she went back to the porch pump and filled the basin with water. Pulling a washcloth off a nail that was pounded in the wall above the table just for that purpose, she scrubbed her face. The mirror caught the image of the big cabin, as seen through the grainy screen of the porch. She looked back at her own reflection. The cowlick on the right side of her bangs made her hair stand straight up. *Stupid cowlick.* She tried to paste it down with water. *Forget it. It's summer at the lake. Hair's not a problem here.*

She went into the cabin and pulled the notebook out that was hidden under her pillow. She'd been keeping it up pretty faithfully—ever since she and Howard had kept track of the "clues" last month that led to the discovery of Dad's cousin, Peter. Lately she'd just written her thoughts, more or less. Sitting down again on the cabin's porch steps, she wrote:

Yesterday, Mum surprised us by saying we had to go to the airport in Calgary. Only Howard, me, and baby Barry went. All she would tell us is that she's been in touch with some distant relative who needed someone to take his 12-year-old son for a while this summer. His name is Gyp—what a weird name, short for Gypsy, which is just as weird. He reminds me of a gypsy. I don't even know yet where he's from. Something like Louis and Anna. I should know, I suppose. I think it's in the United States. He's had so many questions for us, I haven't asked him much about himself yet. Tonight, I guess. He's sleeping in the bed beside the door. I made sure Howard was in the bed between us. It feels kind of weird to have a boy my own age staying in this cabin with us. I think it's going to be okay, though. He made us coffee this morning. I liked it. Dad says all good Scandinavians like coffee. What about Cajun people? That's what he called us. Am I Cajun? Never even heard of it. More later.

Your intimate friend, Norma Jean.

Chapter 2
CABIN GHOSTS AND COONDOGS

The Coleman lantern sat on the table between Howard and Norma Jean's beds. All three children were in pajamas, tucked tightly under flannel sheets and wool blankets. Shadows danced on the clapboard walls and the moon shone through the knotholes.

"I've never had a day like this before," Gyp broke the silence.

Out of the corner of her eye, Norma Jean could see Howard turn to look at her. She glanced back at him and they raised their eyebrows at each other. They'd had a hundred, no, a thousand days just like this: swimming in the lake, riding in the boat, water skiing, eating hamburgers.

"So, why exactly are you here, anyway?" Norma Jean had been waiting all day for Howard to ask that question. But he was being especially stubborn about reading her mind today and she finally decided she had to just blurt it out herself. She stared at the familiar bat-board wall that surrounded the window by her bed while she waited for his answer. She knew every line on that wall. All the knotholes, the variegated wood grains, her and Howard's initials that they had carved when she was only six. And still Gyp didn't answer.

"Gyp? You asleep already?" Howard asked.

"No. Just listening to the crickets and thinking how some things are the same no matter where you live in the world. Crickets, mosquitoes... I like it. My family is REALLY small. In fact it's me. That's it."

"That sounds...really great!" Howard said laughing. Norma Jean ignored him, sat up and turned her back to lean on the cool window sill. She pulled her knees up to her chest and grabbed her shins. Howard also sat up and looked over at Gyp, who was still lying flat in his bed.

After a few moments of silence, Norma Jean said, "You don't have to tell us more if you don't want to. We're glad you're here. I've never seen anyone learn to water ski so quickly and you're fab at making fires," she laughed. "Mum just about had a cow when she brought the hamburgers down from the cabin and the supper fire was all ready to go—grill and everything. She might never let you leave!" She and Howard both laughed.

"I wish..." Gyp rolled over onto his left side and looked at Norma Jean and Howard. "I wish..." he started again. He stared past them, and Norma Jean could see the bright moonlight reflecting in his eyes. Suddenly he sat up. Norma Jean and Howard looked at him.

"Hey, what's that carved in the window frame beside your bed, Norma Jean?"

"Where? You mean here?" She pointed to the top right-hand side of the wooden frame: "H.W.N. and N.J.N. Those are just Howard's and my initials."

"We carved them there when we were kids," Howard continued.

"There." Gyp pointed to some initials carved on the bat-board wall above the window frame.

"Oh those!" Howard laughed. "Those initials belong to ol' B.R.D. Norma Jean and I call him the 'cabin ghost'—B.R.D. Sound out the letters like a word and it says, 'board'. Get it? The initials read 'board'. I know it's not very funny but we thought it up when we were just little kids. We call it our cabin ghost, whose name is Board. We wanted to add our initials to his."

"It kinda makes these digs seem more like our own," Norma Jean explained further.

Gyp got out of the bed and came between Norma Jean and Howard's bed to get the lantern. His blue and white striped flannel pajamas were a little too big and too new. He leaned over Norma Jean's bed and held the lantern up as high as he could, illuminating the initials. "B.R.D." he read. "St. Afan Alive!" He put the lantern back on the table between Howard and Norma Jean's bed, then scampered across the cold floor to his own bed on the other side of the room. He crawled in under his still-warm flannel and wool blankets and yawned.

"What's the big deal?" Howard asked.

"Just coincidence, but those are my initials. My real name is <u>B</u>ernard <u>R</u>ichard <u>D</u>upre." Gyp yawned again, rolled over and started breathing deeply.

Norma Jean and Howard waited for a few moments before they started talking again. When Gyp's breathing had slowed down and a very slight snore had begun, Howard said, "You know what he said to me when we were playing on the the lake today?"

"No, what?" Norma Jean whispered.

"He said that he thinks you're cute!"

Norma Jean hit Howard with her pillow, "He did not, you idiot. What did he really say?" She could feel her face getting red in spite of herself.

"You're right, he didn't say that." Howard threw the pillow back.

"SHHH!" she hissed, "We don't want to wake him up. What did he really say?" She wasn't sure if she wanted Howard to repeat what he'd already said or not. *DID he say that? Oh DANG that Howard. Now I'll NEVER be sure! What if he DID?*

"He said that he has the feeling he's being watched," Howard said.

"What?! That's just silly. There's no one here but us!" Norma Jean said.

Just then the coondog howled. Howard got out of bed, went out on the porch and softly called to Nicky. "Come on, boy! Time to come home. Leave that ol' coondog alone until morning." He waited. Nicky finally came bouncing up the cabin steps and curled up under the rocking chair.

"Norma Jean!" Howard whispered fiercely. "Get out here!" He stepped back until he was hidden in the shadow afforded by the tall spruce tree that was at the north-west corner of the porch.

The urgency in Howard's voice made Norma Jean obey instantly. She put on her slippers and ran to join him. "What?" she whispered back. Howard pulled her into the shadows.

"Look. Over there," he pointed toward Spruce Bay campground. Fifty yards away, on the knoll that separated their two properties, stood the coondog. Standing beside him was a figure, tall and cloaked, looking straight towards Howard and Norma Jean.

"What...who is it?" Norma Jean muffled her voice behind her hand.

"I have no idea," Howard returned. The coondog started to howl again, and Nicky lifted his head and softly whined. "Shhh, Nicky. You stay put, boy. No coondog is gonna take your gopher dreams. Shhh, boy." Nicky put his head back down. Norma Jean and Howard could see the cloaked phantom turn and lift its face to the moon. The hood fell down and Norma Jean said, "That's the old, and I mean REALLY old, lady that lives at Spruce Bay. Someone's great-great-grandmum or something."

The coondog turned and faced the moon and commenced howling anew. The dog then began circling the old lady, bearing right, and she started circling the dog, bearing left...both lifting their faces to the moon.

"They're freaking me out!" Howard whispered. "If she starts howling too, I'M gonna freak out!"

"SHHH! Howard," Norma Jean said, "Just watch!"

And then, abruptly, they turned and walked down the knoll, back toward Spruce Bay. Norma Jean and Howard looked at each other, their eyes shining in the moonlight.

"Creepy!" Howard said. Norma Jean agreed. She walked over to Nicky, patted his head, and then they both ran softly back into the cabin. They could hear Gyp's night-breath as they passed his bed and knew he was sleeping. They sat on the edges of their beds facing each other, their knees almost touching, and stared at each other.

"Howard," Norma Jean finally breathed, "it's time to start our notebook again." She pulled the notebook out from under her pillow, ripped today's diary pages out and took them over to the still smoldering stove. Picking up and using the steel lever that Dad had made, she wedged the round cast iron burner lid up. She dropped the diary pages into the gaping hole and watched as they spit forth yellow flame. "Dear Diary," she whispered, "something more interesting has come up. I'll talk to you later." She sat back down on her bed and looked at Howard.

"Do you always have to be so dramatic?" he said.

Ignoring him, Norma Jean opened up a fresh page in the notebook and wrote:

Clue Number 1: Our B.R.D ghost has a name and he's sleeping in the bed across the cabin. Bernard Richard Dupre.

Clue Number 2: The coondog and the great-great-grandmother from Spruce Bay are watching us and being really, really creepy.

She read them aloud to Howard. "Anything else?" she asked.

"Yeah, turn the lantern off before you go to bed. I'm ready to catch some Z's." He rolled over and immediately started snoring.

Norma Jean did so, then tucked herself back under the warm blankets. She turned toward the window and whispered to herself, "Why oh why, Mr. Gypsy, won't you tell us why you are here." Then she remembered that Gyp had talked in his sleep last night. *The key. Who is asking him if he has the key?* She sat up, pulled the notebook back out and wrote:

Clue Number 3: Gyp is sleep-talking about a key.

She reminded herself to tell Howard in the morning about this new clue.

For the third time that night, she tucked in under her warm blankets. She looked out the window at the tree tops that were silhouetted in the residue of the late Alberta sunset. A big blackbird sat motionless on a fat branch and seemed to stare right into the cabin and straight into Norma Jean's eyes. She sat up in bed and silently swished her hands and arms in its direction. *Get lost you creepy thing!* It didn't move. She laid back down, covered herself up, and turned her back to the window.

If only I could stay awake to listen for more clues...

She slept.

Chapter 3
MYSTERY IN DIXIELAND

Norma Jean woke the next morning and lay still, listening to the robins greet the dawn. Gyp and Howard were still sleeping and she could hear their gentle snores. She put her hands behind her head and let her gaze rest just above the window frame. B.R.D. *Who was he—besides the boy lying in the bed across the room?* She sighed quietly and moved her eyes to the ceiling. She knew those rough wooden rafters like the back of her hand. They held no secrets, revealed no answers, but still she stared at them. The cabin had been built in 1905—it was carved on the porch railing. But who was B.R.D.? Was there another Bernard Richard Dupre who'd lived in this cabin? She sighed again.

"Awful lot of sighing coming from that side of the cabin." Gyp sat up and grinned at Norma Jean. "Wanna learn to make coffee?"

Norma Jean tucked her arms back under her quilt. She sighed again, "I dunno."

Gyp laughed and jumped out of bed. Norma Jean watched out of the corner of her eye until she was sure there was plenty of blue-striped flannel pajama. A flash of something gold around his neck caught her eye.

"What is..."

He grabbed the coffee pot and went to the porch pump.

Maybe I shouldn't ask.

"You are my sunshine, my only sunshine. You make me happy when skies are blue. You'll never know dear, how much I love you..." he sang.

Norma Jean sat up in bed, taking care to adjust her pajamas. She stared at him through the porch screen. His black hair was standing on end but he looked like he hadn't a care in the world. *He's the strangest boy I've ever met.*

"When skies are gray!" Norma Jean shouted. "Gray not blue!"

"Just checkin' to see how Cajun you are. And you're more Cajun than you know!"

The screen door banged and he brought the pot back in and set it on the stove.

Norma Jean glanced over at Howard. Still asleep. *This is going to be an interesting summer.*

Gyp began to coax the banked fire back to life. "Here's what you do, Norma Jean. You fill the coffee pot with water." He glanced over at her and grinned.

She found herself grinning back. "I think I could figure that much out. Why were you singing that?"

"Ah! Can't tell. Old Louisianan secret."

"Yeah, right." She swung her feet across the bed and found the slippers that were waiting on the floor beside it.

"Then you get the fire going." He started whistling through his grin.

"Then you put the coffee pot on the stove..." Norma Jean said as she rolled her eyes.

"No, I've already done that, see?" He adjusted the pot, his eyes dancing. "Then you wait for the water to boil."

She hadn't really planned to like this boy, but...

"I'm getting dressed." She grabbed the clothes she'd laid on the end of her bed the night before and disappeared into the roomy closet, "Don't come in!" she yelled. *Why'd I say that? Of course, he's not coming in.*

"Actually, it's a song my great-grand-mère used to sing to me."

Norma Jean paused and looked at the closet side of the curtain. "Whaddya mean, 'used to'?"

"She's dead, of course. Older than an alligator washboard."

"How come you didn't call her Grandma?"

"It's the Cajun way, of course. Don't you call your mom's mom, 'Grand-mère'?"

"Nope. Why should we?"

"Boy, you really don't know very much, do you?"

Norma Jean chose to ignore him.

Gyp started whistling and she heard the screen door bang.

"*Frère Jacques, Frère Jacques*," he began singing. "*Dormez-vous? Dormez-vous? Sonnez les matines! Sonnez les matines!*"

"All right! All right, already!" Norma Jean yelled from the closet. "I'm NOT sleeping..."

"WHO COULD?" Howard cajoled from his bed, then rolled over and started snoring again.

Norma Jean continued, "I HEAR the morning bells ringing. And I'm NOT Brother John. YOU however are gonna be din, dan, don!"

She pulled on her cut-offs and grabbed her T-shirt—same T-shirt that she'd worn yesterday. She stopped with one arm through the sleeve. Just a glimpse in the mirror at her early morning reflection told her that Mum was right. She should start wearing that bra they'd bought at the Saan Store. Sighing yet again, she opened a dresser drawer. *I know it's in here somewhere.* She pulled it out looking at it with a mixture of disgust and intrigue. *Why on earth does*

HE make me think of bras? There he goes singing again. At the last minute she changed her mind on yesterday's T-shirt and pulled on a clean yellow one. Yanking the closet curtain open, she walked straight to the porch to brush her hair.

Gyp raised his eyes to watch her and then called, "When the water's boiling you measure out one tablespoon of coffee for every cup of water you've put in the pot."

"Uh-huh." She looked in the mirror as she pulled her hair into a ponytail. *Guess I'd better take some shampoo to the lake today.* "Then what?"

"Let it boil for three minutes." He reached to the paper-lined shelf and pulled down three mismatched coffee mugs and a covered bowl of sugar cubes. "Hey, Norma Jean, bring a little cold water back in with you."

"OK." She glanced around for something to carry it in. "Can I use the dog's bowl?"

"Sure! We'll call it *Nick's Special Brew.* Gotta nice ring to it."

"Well, you didn't say you were going to put it in the coffee." She rinsed the cup they used for brushing their teeth and filled it with water. She pushed the screen door open with her hip, holding the cup with one hand and pressing down that infernal cowlick with the other.

"Don't worry about your cowlick. It's cute. Then you pour a splash of cold water into the coffee so all the grounds sink to the bottom." He suited the action to his words.

35

Norma Jean stood behind him, hoping with all her heart he wouldn't turn around in time to see the blush of pink race across her face.

"And then you pounce on Howie." Gyp made a dive for Howard's bed.

Norma Jean watched them for a few seconds then went to the stove. "Then you pour the coffee and go sit on the porch and drink it while the stupid boys have a pillow fight," she said to no one.

She sat on the porch steps, letting the eastern sun warm her face. Closing her eyes, she listened to the sounds of the morning: the hum of a distant motor boat, Nicky's bark, and the rustle of the breeze in the lilac bushes. She gazed over to the big cabin and thought about breakfast.

Swirling the coffee grounds with the remains of the coffee, she threw them onto grass. She left the cup on the porch step and walked the short distance to the big cabin.

"Morning!" Elbowing Keith out of the way, she grabbed a plate, stood beside the stove and held it out, waiting for the next pancake. Just as Mum was about to put it on her plate, Keith put his plate on top of hers and the pancake landed on it. They began their daily ritual of push/shove, push/shove. For some reason, they both found it amusing. Norma Jean tried again...Success! A whole-wheat blueberry pancake was covering her entire plate.

"Thanks, Mum." She looked for Dad and then pushed her way into the circle of siblings that were already seated at the long oak table. "Hey, Dad, are you going to the farm today?"

"Uh-huh."

"Why don't you take Gyp and Howard with you?"

Dad looked at Norma Jean and smiled. After a slight pause, he said, "Good idea. Gyp's been wanting to see the farm. We're cultivating the Home Place, north quarter. He can ride along on the tractor and then they can swim in the dugout."

Norma Jean smiled her thanks. No need to tell Dad she needed a day to herself—he knew. Besides, there were just a few things she wanted to do...by herself... "And Dad," she continued, "may I have a dollar?"

Dad pulled out his wallet and using his nickname for her, said "What's going on, Yommpy-Doodle-Dandy?"

"I'd like to go to the store at Spruce Bay and get a pop. Is that okay?"

"Sure is. Bring one back for me, too. Here's 50 cents. Orange Crush, please."

"I'm not coming right back, Dad. Is that groovy?" she smiled big.

He looked at Norma Jean and laughed. "Never mind. You go on and spend the whole groovy day alone, drinking your Grape Crush whenever and wherever you want. Don't bother about me." He tousled her blond bangs and went to get Howard and Gyp.

Ever since Gyp had used the phrase *grand-mère,* Norma Jean had been thinking. She was sure she'd heard that name used before.

Norma Jean ran down the tree-lined path that led to the lake. Where she usually took the right turn to their family's private beach, she turned left and headed toward the public campground, called Spruce Bay. She jogged easily over tree roots, ducking under spruce tree boughs, past the bear cave, and entered the campground. She followed the trail as it wound through the cabin area, past the trailers and campers, past the boat dock, past the swing sets, and then to the front of the tiny country store and lunch counter. She was hoping Dixie was working today. Dixie's family owned the campground and they all seemed to work the store on any given day.

"Hey there, Norma Jean! Where've you been?" Dixie leaned her ample 16-year-old bosom on the lunch counter and Norma Jean sat on a stool facing her.

"Hi, Dixie! Been busy swimming of course! Dad bought us new flippers this year and Howard and I have been swimming to the cove every day. Plus, we've got this boy here visiting...from La-whez-e-anna." Norma Jean said the state's name slowly and watched Dixie carefully to see if she had any response.

"Louisiana! Well, la-de-da. Is he brewing chicory and calling it coffee and frying up catfish for ya?"

Norma Jean just stared at her.

"What's the matter?" Dixie asked, pulling a Grape Crush out of the ice box and handing it to her. Norma Jean grabbed the bottle opener that hung by a string at the end of the counter and popped off the cap. "Well...I don't know..." she started.

Dixie laughed. "My *practically* blind great-great-grand-mère is from Louisiana." Dixie leaned towards Norma Jean, her long, black hair falling forward, off her shoulders and onto the lunch counter. She lowered her voice.

"She creeps me out, to tell you the truth. Always hiding in that little hut behind that stand of spruce trees..."

Norma Jean looked to where Dixie was pointing.

"Where?" Norma Jean asked.

"There," Dixie pointed again, "up the lake shore a bit."

Still Norma Jean sought to find the hut, searching the area earnestly with her eyes.

"I know," Dixie confirmed Norma Jean's confusion. "Most people don't even know she's there. But she is. And she's scary as hell." Dixie's parents let her use those kind of words, and oh man, did Dixie like to use them.

Norma Jean still couldn't see anything that resembled a hut. There wasn't much that missed Norma Jean's observations and this piece in the puzzle of Spruce Bay truly surprised her.

"Would you like an ice-cold Coke, Grand-père?" Dixie called to the older man who was docking a rowboat on the shore.

Dixie cozied up to Norma Jean again, "Great-great-grand-mère is furious at Grand- père because he trimmed some of the trees around her hut. You used to not be able to see anything."

Grand-mère, Grand-père...THIS is where I've heard these terms before. So, Gyp and the Lablanc family from Spruce Bay are ALSO Cajun. I wonder if Mum knows...

Dixie opened the cooler, pulled out a bottle of Coke, opened it, and set it on the counter ready for her grand-père to retrieve.

Norma Jean had never spoken to Dixie's Grand-père, much less come within 25 feet of him. She shrank, ever so slightly, into the red vinyl-topped stool, and swerved it ever so slightly so that her right shoulder guarded the rest of her body. She had no reason to be afraid of him, but still, his dark complexion, bushy black eyebrows, giant mustache, and bulging biceps frightened her just a little. He nodded once to Dixie, put the rowboat lead rope around a rock and walked up to the counter.

"Thanks, Sis," he said roughly to Dixie. He turned to walk away, then paused and turned around, looking Norma Jean straight in the eye.

"Tell that boy that the Leblanc family send their regards and that there's no gris-gris nonsense in these parts." And with that, he was gone.

Norma Jean looked at Dixie, wide-eyed, "What...?"

"Oh, don't worry about him. He's a little odd. Harmless, but odd."

Norma Jean heard the coondog howl. "Nice to see you Dixie." She shivered, jumped off the stool and put the empty pop bottle in the wire rack.

"You too, Norma Jean. Tell those brothers of yours to stop working so hard and come over for a milkshake. I'll make them the thickest strawberry shake they ever did see."

"I'll tell them," Norma Jean responded, even though she knew none of them would be thrilled. Dixie just wasn't their kind of girl. Norma Jean knew nothing about how they picked their girlfriends, but she knew Dixie was never going to be one.

Norma Jean ran slowly back through the campground to the trail. *Maybe wearing a bra is a good thing after all.* She felt weird even thinking it. But more importantly, she needed to think about Great-great-grandmère, and Grandpère. That Dixie's family could share the same roots as her family was a thought that Norma Jean would never, ever, in her wildest imaginations, have imagined.

Before she entered the trailhead, she turned around and scrutinized the campground. Walking to the shore of the lake, she kicked off her socks and runners, and waded in up to the bottom of her cut-offs. Slapping off midsummer mosquitoes, she casually gazed down the lake shore toward the great-

great-grandmère's hut. *Just as I thought. We could get there in a* rowboat. And no wonder we've never noticed it. It's completely hidden behind those reeds.

She slowly got out of the water, pretending to enjoy a little splash on a hot day, just in CASE anyone was watching her watch the hut. She knew she was probably being ridiculous, but it made everything seems more exciting. After all, you never know...

***

The rain beat mercilessly against the small cabin's rugged walls. Gyp opened the screen door and stood on the porch watching the lightening storm.

"Does it always rain this hard in Alberta?"

"Only in the summertime—wait 'til the rainbow comes out. It'll be stunning."

"Stunning. That's a good word, Norma Jean. I think I'll start using it. It rains like this in Louisiana too. We've got lots of stuff in common."

Norma Jean was standing beside him. They stood in silence, watching the water pour off the porch roof and dig a hole into the flowerbeds below. Norma Jean glanced at Gyp out of the corner of her eye. *I like this boy. Not LIKE like—I just like him. Well, maybe I LIKE him. I don't know yet. I didn't LIKE him last week when he first came, but now...well, I'm glad he's here.*

Norma Jean hadn't been able to do anything with her new information. They'd had to go to the farm for the last four days and work in the garden.

Gyp had actually LIKED it. He'd wanted to stay there to help Mum pick peas and raspberries, and ride the tractor with Dad when he cultivated the west-quarter.

Of course, he'd discovered the dugout too. Norma Jean had gone to Uncle Reynold's for a night and visited with Uncle Peter. The family was enjoying getting to know this new uncle whose appearance had rocked their world.

Now, thankfully, they were back at the lake. Norma Jean had decided that tonight she would tell Gyp about the notebook and she, and Howard, and Gyp would add her clues. She hoped to not be embarrassed. Somehow she thought it would be okay.

She whispered the clues under her breath:

Clue Number 4: Dixie's family is from Louisiana; Grand-père knows Gyp.

Clue Number 5: What is gris-gris?

Clue Number 6: Great-great-grand-mère lives in a hut, hidden in the spruce grove.

"Hey," she said, elbowing Gyp, "Let's get out the *Risk* game and do an all-dayer." She went back inside the cabin, Gyp following her, and poked at the very needed fire.

"Sure. Whatever *Risk* is. Sounds fun. Howie thinks he's gonna snore the day away. Ha!" He cannonballed himself at Howie's bed and commenced the pillow fight that had become standard morning fare.

Norma Jean rolled her eyes. *God puts me in a family with five brothers and then sends me a BOY to visit for the whole summer. Maybe this isn't as great as I thought.*

Chapter 4
A CAJUN RIDDLE

Norma Jean actually loved a rainy day in the small cabin. Everything was closed in but not claustrophobically. While the boys finished their pillow fight, Norma Jean walked over to the shelf and browsed, for the thousandth time, the mildewed volumes. She'd never read any of them. Her own library books held more appeal than these. But she loved that they were here. Books comforted her. She ran her fingers across their bindings and said softly, "Someday I'll read you. I don't mean anything by it. I'm not ignoring you. Really." She smiled at her own words.

The coffee sat on the hot stove, ready to go. The teapot sat right beside it. She pulled three mugs off the shelf and poured herself a cup of tea. Mum had insisted she and Howard switch from coffee to tea. Norma Jean didn't mind. She liked tea better anyway. Howard, however, had started mixing the two. He claimed it was delicious. Gyp called it *Nick's Brew*.

She melted butter in the cast iron pan and fried some toast. Brushing the crumbs off the red-checkered tablecloth, she put saskatoon jam, plates, serviettes and knives on the table.

"Come on you guys, let's eat."

The boys untangled themselves and Norma Jean poured coffee, Nick's Brew and her tea. Then, through the noise of the rain, Norma Jean heard a familiar voice calling from the porch.

"Hi!" The screen door opened. Dad stood on the multicoloured braided rug, dripping with water. "Can a guy get a cup of coffee around here?"

"Hi Dad!" Norma Jean jumped up, threw him a towel that was slung across the makeshift clothesline, and pulled another mug off the shelf. "Would you like Gyp's coffee, Nick's Brew, or tea?"

The boys laughed and Howard pushed his cup across the table for Dad to look at.

"Nick's brew," Howard said.

Dad raised his eyebrows and looked at Norma Jean. She just rolled her eyes and said, "Don't even ask."

"Guess I'll have some of Gyp's coffee." Dad sat down on a low-backed wooden chair and pulled it toward the table. "Well, this is nice. Good thing we have a rainy day once in a while. How's it going out here, kids?" He took a gulp of coffee and leaned back in his chair.

"Great!" Howard said. "We're gonna do an all day *Risk* tournament. Wanna join us?"

"Sure don't. Norma Jean always wins and we have to hear about it for weeks afterwards. I'm going into town to look at new cars." He winked. "I sure do love a rainy day. Got any more of that toast?"

"'Course, Dad." Norma Jean put the pan back on the stove and fried Dad a nice thick slice.

Dad reached into his shirt pocket. "I've got mail for you, Gyp. Looks like it's from Nova Scotia."

"Finally! Thanks Uncle." Gyp took the letter and devoured the return address with his eyes. "It's from my Père...my dad."

"Never mind about us, Gyp," Dad said softly. "You go on and read it. Have you tried that wicker chair on the porch yet or have you been so busy swimming, playing, and gardening that you've not sat down? Go on, Son. I've been wanting to check up on these two scallywags and I'm lovin' your coffee."

Gyp got up from the table and took the letter to the porch. Norma Jean could see the side of his face as he sat in the wicker chair and ripped the letter open. She purposely stopped looking at him. Somehow it didn't seem right that he should be watched. Besides that, Dad was here. She had lots to say to him. Unless she went to the farm with him and spent the day riding the swather, she hardly ever saw him. Soon harvest would be over and Dad's long work hours would cease. The whole family loved a rainy day once in a while.

Fifteen minutes later, Dad pushed his chair back from the table. "Thanks for breakfast." He stood up, leaned toward Norma Jean and Howard and whispered, "And thanks for sharing the cabin. You two kids are exactly what Gyp needs this summer." He pushed the screen door open and met Gyp as he passed through. "You all right, Son?"

Norma Jean noticed that Gyp's usually bright black eyes were even brighter. *Could it be tears?*

"Thanks, Uncle. I'm fine."

Dad touched his shoulder, glanced back at his kids and ran through the rain, back to the big cabin.

Norma Jean filled Gyp's coffee cup. "Want some more toast?" she asked.

"By the beard of St. George that's exactly what I need." He grinned and the tension left the room.

Just then the screen door pushed open and Mum entered the cabin.

"Mum?" Norma Jean and Howard both said. Mum hung the dripping wet yellow rain coat on a nail beside the stove, and shook out her permed brown curls. Howard helped her pull off her rain boots and Norma Jean handed her a pair of slippers that Bedstemor had made especially for the cabin.

"We've got tea, coffee, Nick's Brew...you don't want that...toast, and...well, that's all," Norma Jean said to her, smiling.

"Thanks, Honey, tea is absolutely perfect." She took the steaming mug from Norma Jean.

Norma Jean pulled out the chair that she and Howard called the *B.R.D. Ghost Chair*. It seemed appropriate that Mum sat in it this morning. It was painted bright blue and was the only one of its kind. Mum had told them it had belonged to one of her relatives.

"Would you like to prop your feet in front of the stove, Mum?" Howard asked.

"Would I?!" Mum lifted her feet and placed them on the small wooden milk stool that Howard slipped under them. "Ah. I can see why you kids love this small cabin. It's SO cozy. Mind if I move in?"

Howard and Norma Jean looked at each other. Mum laughed, "Don't worry, I'm just kidding. I do remember staying here when I was a child." She looked around the room. "It really hasn't changed much."

Norma Jean walked over to the window that was on the side of her bed and pointed to B.R.D. "Mum, these are Gyp's initials. That's weird, isn't it?"

"Not really," said Mum. "That name has been handed down in my family for generations. *That* B.R.D. was my great-uncle. He lived here until his wife died in childbirth, then he disappeared. I inherited this property a generation later. But I do remember being here..." she smiled. "But what IS weird is that every Dupre that is named Bernard

Richard has the nickname, Gypsy. Can you guess why?"

They all shook their heads, even Gyp.

"Really, Gyp?" Mum said, "You don't know the legend?"

"I suppose I should considering my folks are Acadian history buffs, but honest, Auntie, I don't."

"Well, something VERY serious happened in 1802, about 50 years after *Le Grand Dérangement*...

"The what?" Howard asked.

"*LeGrand Dérangement* means expulsion," Gyp said, "That much I know."

"That's right, the Expulsion of the Acadian people from Nova Scotia to Louisiana," she said.

"Well, that's serious, but what happened 50 years later?" Howard asked.

"An Acadian named Bernard Richard Dupre married a woman named Viollca Mala Copper," she winked.

"Seriously weird name, but...?" Howard probed.

"She was a gypsy, kicked out of France just as our people had been kicked out of Nova Scotia," Mum said. "Ever since then, 'Gypsy' has been a nickname for every boy named Bernard Richard Dupre. I'm sure it was meant to be a slight to the original B.R.D.; after all, the Acadian people had to fight hard to keep their traditions and their faith. Marrying a gypsy was NOT what you might call, proper. Now, it's just fun family folklore. And, as you see, my great-uncle had that name."

"Well, congratulations, Bernard," Howard said. "Lucky you! You get to be called Gypsy. I wish that was MY name. Mum, why didn't you name ME that?"

"Never mind, Howie," Gyp said. "You wouldn't look like Howie, with the name Gypsy."

"Suppose so." Howard got up from his perch on the bed, walked to the table and grabbed another piece of buttered toast. "You don't mind if I eat while we talk, do you?"

"Eat at the table, Howard. Don't get crumbs in the bed," Norma Jean said.

Howard looked at Mum and she smiled but said nothing. "Whaddya care if I get crumbs in the bed Miss Bossy Pants? I'm the only one who sleeps in it!" he said, moving back to his bed and sitting with the pillow propped against the wall. "Okay. Ready," he continued, smacking his lips.

Norma Jean sighed, but stayed silent.

"So, I'm anxious to hear how your parents' project is going, Gyp? Is there a report in the letter?" Mum asked. "Go ahead and fill your coffee cup first, if you'd like," she smiled.

Gyp smiled back and went to the stove, poured the acrid liquid into his cup and returned to sit beside Mum.

"How come we had to switch to tea, Mum?" Howard asked.

"You're just full of questions this morning, aren't you Howard," Mum said. "Chicory coffee is the Cajun way. I want Gyp to feel at home here while his parents are in Nova Scotia all summer.

"How come we've never had Gyp here before or even ever heard of him?" Howard asked Mum, while looking at Gyp.

"It's certainly about time, isn't it? And I *have* talked about these Cajun relatives, but I suspect you've been building tree forts, or following Norma Jean through ditches..." Mum said.

"I don't follow Norma Jean, she follows me!" Howard said, purposely dropping crumbs on his bed.

Mum laughed. "It doesn't matter who does the following on any given day, the point is you're busy with your own sweet life, and me...well, I actually have one too, believe it or not. You know those letters I get every once in a while? Since it's your and Norma Jean's job to get the mail, I'm sure you've noticed those odd stamps from Louisiana; those are from Gyp's dad, and we've become pen pals. I've know Gyp's dad, through letters, since before any of you were born and even before he was married to Gyp's mum," she smiled at Gyp, "although they were dating. They met at the museum, I believe." Gyp nodded. "I've never met either of them but we know each other, and of course, Gyp's dad and I are distantly related."

"I didn't know adults could have pen pals," Howard said. "Who'd wanna write a letter..."

"Never mind, Howard," Mum interrupted him. "Lots of people; lots of interests. Makes the world go 'round."

"Makes the...?" Howard started.

"Never mind, Howard!" Norma Jean almost shouted in exasperation. "Please, Mum, keep talking!"

Howard looked at her and dropped some more crumbs on his bed.

Gyp laughed, "Maybe I'll be so entertained here that I'll forget to be homesick," he said.

Ah, THAT'S what those glistening eyes were about. He's homesick. Well, I suppose I would be too.

"I certainly believe that's possible, Gyp," Mum laughed. "And I hope it happens."

"So, anyway, Mum... the Acadians...?" Norma Jean encouraged. She liked history. And she remembered a poem: *Evangelina, A Tale of Acadia,* by Henry Longfellow. No, she didn't like, she LOVED this stuff.

"The Acadian people, who were French Catholics, were pushed out of the Maritime provinces in Canada and forced to flee the country."

"Why?" Howard asked.

Okay, so maybe this time it was all right that Howard was a questioner.

"The Acadian people did not want to pledge allegiance to the King of England. And so, they had to leave. Our ancestors were amongst the thousands that exited the country. Can you guess where they went?"

"Mum, is this just a history lesson? School's over," Howard said.

"Be quiet, Howard," Norma Jean mothered. "I can guess, Mum. Louisiana. Am I right?"

"Right you are, Norma Jean," Mum said. "Don't worry, Howard, no tests, no reading, no reports. Just a fun summer with a relative from Louisiana."

"Cool!" Howard shouted.

"Cool?" Mum asked.

"Yeah, I heard Allan say it. It's cool!" Howard laughed.

Mum laughed too. "Very well, then. Cool it is."

"So, why have you been in touch with Gyp's family since before he, and Norma Jean and I, were born?"

"Well," Mum adjusted the stool a little closer to the stove, "on my wedding day my mum, actually, I should use the Cajun term and call her, Mère, gave me the *Cajun Treasure* that every oldest child gets on the day of her marriage. It was a French Bible—mine is dated 1730—and tucked inside it was a letter of sorts, maybe just a note...or some folk have even called it a riddle."

"What's it say?" Norma Jean interrupted.

"It said," and Mum quoted by heart:
My dear Marie,
You are the order to my past;
You are the joy of my present;
You are the hope for my future.

The key to future happiness
is remembering your past.
If you do not, the key is not for you,
but for another.
Love, Père

"Cool!" Howard said.

"So, anyway, the contents of that oldest child's gift made me wonder if ALL my family got the same thing. I decided to try and get in touch with my Louisiana family with whom we'd lost touch...oh probably generations ago. I sent a letter to the museum in Lafayette and the curator there knew Gyp's father and mother. Both of them are active volunteers in the Acadian community and often work at the museum helping to archive the artifacts that are unearthed both in Louisiana and in Nova Scotia. He gave my letter to him. We've been corresponding ever since."

"And my folks are IN Nova Scotia right now." Gyp said.

Norma Jean was happy that he finally felt comfortable to talk about this.

"They are opening a new museum in St. Croix," he continued, "the original site of one of the first Acadian villages: Trahan. This hamlet was burned down at the time of *Le Grand Dérangement*. Mom and Dad are sort of experts on Acadian artifacts and they asked them to come and help...for the whole summer. But it's *très bon*." he smiled at Mum.

"Glad to hear it, Gyp. And this is enough for one day. What does the rest of your rainy day hold?"

"RISK!" Norma Jean and Howard both shouted together.

"ALL DAY!" Howard continued, "Can you bring us lunch, Mum?"

She looked them over, laughed, and said, "I'll send Kathy down with something for you. In fact, why don't you ask her to play?"

Norma Jean looked at Mum. Her sister was okay, but Norma Jean didn't really want to spill the beans about the notebook and the clues in front of Kathy. *Do I have to?*

"Never mind," Mum said. "I think Kathy is baking saskatoon muffins anyway, and she'd love to have someone eat them. We'll send some down."

"We picked those saskatoons," Howard said to Gyp.

"Saskatoons?" he asked.

"You'll see...just wait," Norma Jean smiled. "Prairie deliciousness. Something you don't know anything about in that sissy Louise and Anna land you're from."

"Oh, splendid!" Gyp said as he threw a pillow at Norma Jean.

Mum got up, "Okay, now's the time for me to do *Le Grand Dérangement*!" she pulled on her boots and retrieved her raincoat.

"But, Mum!" Norma Jean laughed. "You forgot to do what you came here for!"

"Oh, of course, how's the project in Nova Scotia going?" Mum looked at Gyp.

"*Bon!*" Gyp said, "They've unearthed an artifact that neither Mom nor Dad have ever seen before, and that's saying something," he said proudly, "a great big key!"

"Sounds interesting!" Mum said.

"Oh! And another thing, Mum," Norma Jean said, "when I was having a pop with Dixie at Spruce Bay, her g*rand-père* gave me a message, and this is it EXACTLY: 'Tell that boy that the Leblanc family send their regards and that there's no gris-gris nonsense in these parts anymore.'"

Mum laughed, "Okay, thanks, Norma Jean. I'll be sure to keep that in mind."

"But what does he mean?" Howard asked.

"Oh, I know this one," Gyp smiled. "No *gris-gris* means no *omens.*"

"Oh," was all that Norma Jean could think to say.

"I'll see you at supper, kids," and Mum was out the door, into the pouring rain.

Norma Jean, Howard, and Gyp went to the leaky-roofed porch and did the dishes together. The old banter returned and the pounding rain afforded antics for the boys to annoy Norma Jean. Inside the cabin again, they pulled the towels from the clothes line, dried off and Norma Jean withdrew the *Risk* game from the cupboard.

"And now, Mr. Bernard Richard Dupre, I'm going to rule the world. Muahaha!"

Gyp grinned at them and then looked heavenward. "Oh Holy Saint Candida. Help me in my hour of need."

"Who's he?" Howard asked.

"Seventh Century saint." Gyp looked at Howard and Norma Jean, his black eyes flashing. "Martyred by pagans."

In the middle of struggling for world dominance, Norma Jean remembered the notebook. *Oh well, if it's still raining tomorrow, I can tell them at breakfast. BUT it IS odd that Gyp was sleep-talking about a KEY before he got the letter from his parents that told him they FOUND a key...*

Once again she whispered the clues to herself:
Clue Number 7: BRD is Mum's great-uncle; his nickname was Gypsy.
Clue Number 8: Key—Gyp dreams about one; Gyp's parents find one; Mum's riddle has one. Why?
Clue Number 9: *Gris-gris* means OMENS.

Chapter 5
NICKY THE FLAG-BEARER

"What's that smell?" Norma Jean sat up on the side of her bed, glad to see the front door of the cabin open and the rain stopped.

"It's chicory for our coffee. Dad sent it to your mum. I was up at the big cabin this morning and your mum gave me some for my coffee." Gyp was pulling a mug from the shelf. "Too bad you stopped drinking coffee. I'd let you try some. Yup, that's really too bad. Ground root of the endive plant, that's chicory. Man, I'm sorry you can't have some," he grinned.

Norma Jean walked out to the front porch, ignoring his banter. Gyp had been here long enough now for her to be used to walking around in her pajamas. *But, sheesh, he sure is into his coffee.* She smiled in spite of herself.

The morning sun made the whole world feel delicious. Anything can happen in a day, and the sun made the possibilities seem endless. She heard Howard and Gyp having their requisite pillow fight.

The outhouse was calling her name and she put on her runners. A large blackbird was perched on the peaked outhouse roof and Norma Jean tried to shoo it away.

"Go on, you big black blackbird. Take your swagger someplace else." He lifted his wings and vaulted a few feet off the roof, then landed again, his beady black eyes staring straight into Norma Jean's. "I said, SHOO!" she clapped her hands and yelled. The bird stayed steady. *Oh well, you stupid thing. I've gotta pee.* She went into the mothballed outhouse. The big bird began pecking, cawing, screeching, and squawking. "I said, 'GO AWAY!!!'" Norma Jean yelled at the top of her lungs. She could hear Howard and Gyp running toward the outhouse. "Hey, guys!" she yelled, "get rid of that dumb bird, would ya?"

"Hey, you thick-headed blackbird! Move on!" Gyp called. "We don't have what you need here." The blackbird turned his inky eyes to Gyp. "*Laisse-la-tranquille!*" Gyp yelled. "*Rentre chez toi!*" Immediately, the blackbird lifted his meaty body and flew away.

Norma Jean exited the outhouse. "Phew. Thanks. What was that all about? What's that creepy bird doing here? And what did you say to it?" She walked back through the long grass and joined Howard and Gyp on the porch stairs. They were both dressed already. "Wait, as soon as I get dressed, I want to call a meeting of the three musketeers."

"There she goes, Gyp," Howard mocked. "She's got something up her sleeve and your summer just got a whole lot more interesting."

"*Laissez les bons temps rouler*!" Gyp shouted and he and Howard commenced a mock sword fight.

"Let the good times roll!" Howard repeated in English.

Fifteen minutes later, they were sitting at the kitchen table, buttered toast, jam, tea, and chicory coffee laid out in front of them. Norma Jean reached onto her lap and then placed the notebook onto the table.

"This," she said, looking at Gyp, "is Howard's and my notebook."

Gyp didn't laugh, but looked at them with steady eyes and somber face.

Encouraged, Norma Jean continued. "Sometimes things happen around here and we need an organized way to keep track of it."

Gyp nodded. Howard took Norma Jean's toast and began eating it.

"Sometime this summer you will meet our Uncle Peter. He's only our Uncle Peter because Howard and I kept this notebook."

Howard said, "Are you going to eat your toast?" Gyp shook his head, not taking his eyes off Norma Jean.

"Gyp, it's time to show you what Howard and I have already written in our notebook." Norma Jean opened it, and shoved it across the table to Gyp. He read aloud:

<u>Clue Number 1:</u> Our B.R.D. Ghost has a name and he's sleeping in the bed across the room. Bernard Richard Dupre.

<u>Clue Number 2:</u> The coondog and the great-great-grandmother from Spruce Bay are watching us and being really, really creepy.

<u>Clue Number 3:</u> Gyp is sleep-talking about a key.

Gyp jerked his head up, "WHAT? I was sleep-talking?"

Howard put down his toast. "I haven't heard Gyp sleep-talking."

"As if you would," Norma Jean said to Howard. She turned to Gyp, "There's LOTS of things to talk about. So, first things first. What did you say to that blackbird out there?"

"That's the FIRST thing?" Gyp asked Norma Jean.

"Well, it could be. Yes. Let's make that the first thing," she responded.

"Okay, but I think it's all connected to your other clues," he said. "Blackbirds, Grand-mère's, coondogs...it's all connected. I'd like you to explain some of these clues first. If you don't mind," he smiled at Norma Jean.

"Yeah, you've added some since we did this, Norma Jean," Howard said.

Norma Jean poured some more tea into her favorite thick glass mug—the one that said HIAWATHA on it. "Okay, let's take Clue Number one first: Don't you think it's odd that this cabin had a B.R.D. living in it two generations ago, and now you're here, AND your parents have to figure out some kind of Dupre mystery?"

"I guess it could be odd, or not," Gyp said.

"Well, Norma Jean will CHOOSE to make it ODD whether is or not," Howard grinned at Gyp. "But it's true that after you went to sleep one night, Norma Jean and I could see the creepy great-great-grandmother and her coondog standing on that hill," he pointed out the cabin door, "staring at us!"

"That's Clue Number two. And number three..." Norma Jean began.

"I was sleep-talking about a key," Gyp said quietly.

"Yeah, why?" Norma Jean asked him.

Gyp got up from the table, went to his bed and dragged his black leather travel bag from under it. He rummaged inside until he found a book, a French Bible, that he brought back to the table. He extracted a folded piece of paper, smoothed it, and laid it on the table. "This is why I've been having that dream." He pointed to the paper. Norma Jean and Howard leaned forward.

"It's that...riddle that Mum knew. The one she got on her wedding day," Norma Jean said.

"How'd you get it?" Howard asked. "You married already?" he laughed.

"Well..." Gyp glanced around the cabin, "I guess I stole it."

"You what?" Norma Jean asked.

"I stole it," he said.

Norma Jean looked at him. "Start talking," she said.

"All right. I wasn't very happy that my parents went off to Nova Scotia for the summer without me," he said.

"But don't you like it..." Howard interrupted.

"This was before I KNEW you and before I GOT here. Now, I'm more glad than ever I didn't go with them. I've been at the museum a lot with my folks and have heard a LOT of talk about their trip. The one thing that kept getting mentioned is that they've got to find the key to the Bernard Richard Dupre mystery, and they always pointed to this letter."

"So, is this why you've been dreaming about the KEY?" Norma Jean asked Gyp.

"I guess so. Sorta weird, I know," he said.

"So, do you think the key they spoke about in your letter is the big key to the Dupre mystery?" Norma Jean asked.

"It COULD be, but I'm not sure," Gyp said.

"Why?" asked Howard.

"Because there was a whole lotta talk about the Bernard Richard Dupre, who had ended up in Alberta, having a key to some kind of Acadian treasure...and THAT'S why I stole the letter, or riddle, whatever you wanna call it. I thought maybe I could help Mom and Dad. I mean since I had to come here and all...plus, I was mad. I could have just copied the letter, but...I was mad that they left me behind," he added sheepishly.

"Okay," Norma Jean said, choosing to ignore Gyp's great confession, "we are going to add that letter to our notebook with the clue: 'Clue number 10: Gyp and Mum have the same riddle.' I just KNEW there was something mysterious about those B.R.D. initials and now we know he's connected to some kind of mystery involving a KEY. I just KNEW it!" Norma Jean's blue eyes shone.

She picked up a pen. "And we also need to change 'Clue Number 3: Gyp is sleep-talking about a key' to: Clue Number 3: OUR B.R.D. is involved in a mystery that involves a KEY." She wrote this out as quickly as possible, the boys watching her.

"Cool!" Howard said.

"And now, I'll tell you what happened at Spruce Bay the day you guys went to the farm," Norma Jean continued.

Howard got up and stove-toasted some more bread while Norma Jean was talking.

"I was talking to Dixie about you, Gyp, and she told me that HER family is from Louisiana, and that that creepy old grandmother lady, whom she calls *great-great-grandmère* lives in a hut along the shoreline that I've NEVER SEEN BEFORE!"

"So?" Gyp asked.

"What? There's a hut behind those reeds?" Howard sat back down at the table.

"Yes," Norma Jean replied. "And that old coondog is hers. Dixie is even creeped out by her."

"I don't see what's so weird about all that," Gyp said.

"Except YOU didn't see her staring..."

"And Dixie said she's *practically* blind," Norma Jean interrupted.

"Yeah. She was staring at us that night, with her dog howling at the moon. We NEVER see her and now she turns up here in the dead of night?! Creepy, man," Howard said.

"Okay, that is creepy, but still, not enough for the notebook," Gyp pressed. He leaned over the table and picked up the letter. As he did so the medallion he wore around his neck fell out from under his shirt. As he reached up to tuck it back in, Norma Jean stopped him.

"Hey, what is that?" she asked.

Gyp pulled it out. "It's the Acadian motto," he said, "*L'union fait la force*, or in English: *Strength through Unity*. Supposedly, it belonged to my great-great-grand-père."

"Cool!" Howard said, again.

"Yeah, it is," Norma Jean agreed. She went on, "THEN there's that message that Dixie's Grand-père, whom I've NEVER heard say two words before, told me to give you: 'Tell that boy that the Leblanc family send their regards and that there's no gris-gris nonsense in these parts anymore.' Mum just laughed at it, but what's THAT supposed to mean?"

They all sat silent for a moment, looking at each other. Suddenly, the peaceful morning was broken by Nicky bounding up the steps to the cabin, barking furiously. He stood at the door, looking in, wagging his tail and whining.

"All right, boy," Howard said, "You need some water?" He got up and pushed the screen door open. "Hey, what's this you got here, Nicky? Where you been, boy? All tangled up in something, it looks like." Howard reached down and pulled a string off Nicky's fine black coat. "What the...?"

Norma Jean and Gyp opened the screen door and joined him.

"Whaddya make of this?" Howard asked them. He held up the string that had been wrapped around Nicky's body. Attached to it was a narrow strip of blue silk cloth, embossed with a star, and surrounded by rays. Underneath the star was a vessel in full sail with the word "Acadia" on a flag.

"This is the Acadian insignia!" Gyp said, "Look, see the words on the bottom...here..." he pointed, "*L'union fait la force*, and the whole thing is crowned with a red and white rosette." He traced the top of the cloth with his fingers and then pulled his medallion back out from under his shirt. "It's the same. But WHY does Nicky have this tied around his body?"

Howard was pumping water for Nicky and putting it into his bowl. "Here you go, boy. Where you been, eh? Come on, you'd better tell us," he reached down and rubbed his belly. "Drink up, you ol' coondog hunter you."

Norma Jean ran back into the cabin. "Come on, guys. That's enough! We need to go investigate a certain hut in a certain reed-covered cove. Now!" She was grabbing bread and already had sandwiches on the go by the time Howard and Gyp had come back in the cabin. "Howard, go get some muffins from the big cabin and tell Mum that we are...that we are...," she hesitated.

"Going for a rowboat ride with Gyp. Because that's what we're doing," Howard said as he ran down the steps. "Come on, Nicky boy! Come on!" Nicky trotted after him, tail wagging.

"Meet us at the lake!" Norma Jean called after him. "And get a pickle jar of water, too! And put your swim trunks on!"

"Got it and already done!" Howard yelled back. "And Norma Jean, put this in the notebook— Clue Number 11: Nicky brings us a message!"

Norma Jean ran back into the cabin and did as Howard instructed. The notebook was filling up fast.

Gyp had gone back to his rucksack and was filling his pockets with stuff. Norma Jean didn't bother to ask. He could take whatever he wanted to. She, however, would take the pair of binoculars she'd grabbed from their fort several days ago. "Don't forget your swim trunks," she said to him. He pulled down the corner of his shorts to show her his green bathing suit. "I'm ready for anything!" he said.

Norma Jean went into the closet and put on her yellow-flowered one-piece bathing suit under her shorts and T-shirt. *It's gonna feel soooo good to get in the lake.*

Everything loaded into a basket, Gyp and Norma Jean took the trail down to the lake. No one was at the beach yet. Dad and the boys were at the farm and wouldn't be back until supper time. Mum, Kathy, and baby Barry were at the big cabin, making jam with the wild gooseberries they had found in the ditch at the entrance to the property.

The beach had been made by Dad and his tractor, his truck, and his brawn. Not that they hadn't all helped, they had, but Dad was the brains behind this oasis. The final product boasted a fairly steep lane starting at the hay field where the cabins were, and winding down to the lake. There was room for several cars to park so Bedstemor and Bedstefar didn't have to traverse the steep trail. The beach itself had been pushed and prodded to be about the size of a community outdoor skating rink. Every year, after the ice melt, Dad and the boys put in the pier, using sledge hammers of enormous size, to pound the pilings into the rocky lake bottom. Norma Jean watched them work but it seemed to her that everything just magically appeared every summer: pier, equipment shed, fire ring, motor boats, rowboats, lawn chairs. That she enjoyed the fruit of their labour, was undisputed. She LOVED the lake.

Howard was already there, and was getting their flippers out of the shed. There were enough pairs for each to have one. And they were brand new. He hooked three life jackets onto a rowboat paddle and walked down the pier.

"The barley was selling high this winter," he smiled as he put his rubber-soled runner on the edge of the shiny new Western Red Cedar rowboat. He dumped the life jackets, paddles and lunch basket into the boat. "Man, this is a great rowboat. We're gonna have so much fun."

Gyp walked to the end of the pier where last year's motor boat was docked. "This is the coolest place I've ever been. I want the summer to last forever."

"Oh yeah, Mum says, 'be careful' and 'be back for supper at 8PM' and..." Howard tried to continue, "I can't remember what else. But that's enough."

They all kicked off their runners and threw them in the boat. Then Gyp untied the knot, "Not bad," he said. "Who's the sailor in the family?"

Howard looked at him, "We all are."

"Yup," Norma Jean agreed, "Now, I'll be the coxswain," she said as she jumped in the back of the boat. "Row, you two!" she laughed.

Howard and Gyp slipped the oars into the oar locks and pushed away from the pier. They were all sitting on their life jackets, more for comfort than any perceived safety.

"Which way, Norma Jean?" Gyp asked.

Norma Jean pointed to a reedy cove that was on the other side of Spruce Bay. "To the hut, slaves! To the hut!" Howard and Gyp, side by side, maneuvered the rowboat away from the dock, being careful not to bang its beautiful new sides, and pointed the vessel toward Spruce Bay.

"Hey," Norma Jean said, "I think we should swing really wide of Spruce Bay so no one sees us rowing by."

"Easy for you to say!" Gyp laughed, "You're not rowing! But the truth of it is, I could row this splendid boat forever. *L'union fait la force,* eh Howard?"

"Strength through Unity!" Norma Jean shouted.

Gyp started to sing, "*You are my sunshine...*"

Norma Jean and Howard joined in...

"*My only sunshine; you make me happy when skies are gray; you'll never know, dear, how much I love you; oh please don't take my sunshine away!*"

"How do you guys know the Louisiana state song?" Gyp said after they had shouted the lyrics to the wild blue yonder. Norma Jean had realized that they were totally blowing their cover, but it didn't matter. It was just so much fun to be in a new rowboat, with Howard, Gyp, and a lunch basket.

"We've always known that song," she said, "Didn't know it was Louise and Anna's favorite song though." She laughed and splashed some water Gyp's way.

"Oh shoot!" Howard said, looking at the shore. "How could we have forgotten Nicky?"

"He'll find us if he wants to," Norma Jean said, "He's the KING of dog-paddle. Besides, he'd just scratch up this mod, new boat."

And then, as if Nicky was listening to them, he started to bark. By this time they were way out in the middle of the lake

"Oh no!" Howard said. "If he tries to swim all the way out here he'll never make it!" Howard stood up in the rowboat and started shouting, "Go home, Nicky! Go home!"

"Let's just send up a flare that says, 'We are in the middle of the lake and we are going to come find your hut...just so you know.' Sit down, Howard!" Norma Jean tugged on his shorts, and Howard tumbled overboard.

That did it for Gyp and he stripped to his swim trunks as fast as you can say *this-isn't-what-I-planned* and was overboard too. What could Norma Jean do but join them. Howard was still worried about Nicky but he had stopped barking so they all decided to make the assumption that he was okay. Besides, the water felt cool, super cool.

Chapter 6
NATURE'S BACKDOOR

After a half hour of splashing and floating, and still no sign of Nicky, Norma Jean convinced the boys it was time to get serious about their destination. They swung back into shore and came up to the reeded cove from the other side of Spruce Bay.

Norma Jean and Howard had never come to this cove. They had their own cove on the other side of their own property. This was one area that they had never explored, nor even thought to. In fact, this cove had never held even a crumb of interest to them...until now, and now it was delicious.

They all quieted down and listened to the splash-pull of the oars, doing what they had been carefully crafted to do. Just before entering the reeds, Norma Jean said, "It's camouflaged somewhere back in these trees; let's look for tree tops that have been trimmed." They continued to pull the boat through the reeds, leaving a swath of broken stems behind them.

Norma Jean dragged the lunch basket closer to her and rummaged around until she found her binoculars. She held them to her eyes, focused them toward the shoreline, and moved her head left and right. "Not a thing," she said, the disappointment noticeable in her voice. She sighed and put them back away. "Oh well, of course I'd EXPECT it to be hidden. What's the point of having a hut if everyone can see it?"

"Wait a sec," Gyp said, "What are we DOING here anyway? What's our plan?" he suppressed a giggle. Norma Jean looked anxiously at Howard, who had never been able to resist a suppressed giggle. *Oh, shoot, here it comes.* Howard started with a small snort, which only encouraged Gyp, who followed with an un-suppressed giggle. Norma Jean had never been very good at resisting the suppressed giggle either. She joined them by laying on the bottom of the boat with the life jacket held over her mouth. Her whole body was chortling so unyieldingly that the boat rocked from side to side.

"Stop it, both of you!" she finally gasped. The boys had stopped rowing and had joined her at the bottom of the boat. Howard opened the lunch basket, pulled out the pickle jar, took a drink and passed it to the others.

"Phew," Gyp said. "That was close. We just about blew our cover."

"And how do you know we didn't?" Norma Jean asked him.

"No coondog barking. That's how, Miss Smarty Pants," he took another drink. "And so, back to my question...what are we DOING here?"

"We're going to explore the hut, of course," Norma Jean said. "We're going in!"

"What? How do you know ol' Creepymère isn't IN her hut, Norma Jean?" Howard said.

"Because...because...if she WAS, we would have heard that coondog barking," she looked at them both smugly.

"Ha!" Gyp said, "Guess ya got us there, Norma Jean. Good one. Okay, so, what's the plan?"

"We're gonna tie the boat over there," she pointed to a small jut-out on the west side of the shoreline. "Then we're gonna wade through the reeds, hiding, until we get close to that patch of cleared shoreline," she stood up in the boat and Howard started to rock it back and forth. "Stop it, Howard!" she grinned, "that patch of shoreline, right there," she pointed east.

Howard and Gyp just looked at her.

"Why not? You afraid of a few reeds, Louise and Anna? OH! That's perfect! My new names for you...which one do you want to be, Howard, Louise or Anna?" she looked at him.

"Ah, Anna, I gue...," he started.

"Howard, you big dork!" Gyp laughed. "Don't answer her!" He cuffed him on top of his head while

Norma Jean muted her laugh once again by biting the bright orange life jacket.

The boys did as Norma Jean directed and they soon had the boat tied off onto a sturdy poplar tree, using a good double loop bowline knot. They were already stripped to their suits and their clothes were stashed in the boat. Norma Jean led the way back into the reeds. The flippers were left in the boat as the reeds were too thick to actually swim through. All of them had put their running shoes back on and were grateful for them once they started in.

"Hey, I'm gonna get stuck in this muck," Howard whispered.

"Shhh. Be quiet, Howard," Norma Jean said. "You can do it."

"Of course I can DO it, Bossy Pants. I just said I was gonna get stuck!" he muttered.

They weaved their way through the reeds that were at least two feet taller than they were. The water came up to their waists at some points, and the bottom of the lake was mucky every step of the way.

Finally, Norma Jean said, "Okay, this is where we turn in. At least, I think it is." They took an immediate right turn and slogged toward the shore.

"Stop!" Norma Jean commanded. The boys obeyed. "I think if we part the reeds right here we can observe while being unobserved," she said.

"She means, let's take a look," Howard said, rolling his eyes to Gyp.

They all crouched down and, using their hands, opened the reeds in front of them.

"I don't see a thing," Howard said. "Are you sure there's a hut here or is it just another one of your..."

"There!" Gyp loud-whispered. "Look at the tree-line... I think there's a small break in it right... there!" he pointed.

"I don't see anything," Howard said.

"Okay, here's what we'll do," Norma Jean said.

"Wait a minute," Howard stood up. "Who made you the boss of us, anyway?"

Gyp suppressed another giggle and before Howard could succumb, Norma Jean jumped in with, "Oh come on, Anna. Just do it."

Gyp dived underwater and Norma Jean and Howard could see bubbles emerging where his body was. When he came up for air he said, "You two have GOT to stop making me laugh!"

Norma Jean and Howard looked at each other and smiled. It was kinda fun having a third kid to make it three musketeers instead of just a couple of siblings.

"As I was saying," Norma Jean continued, "here's what we're gonna do. We're gonna slowly get out of the water and walk along the shore until we see an opening in the trees. Surely..."

"Shirley?" Howard said, "Her name is Creepymère, not Shirley."

This time Gyp pounced on Howard and ducked him under, going under with him. Norma Jean looked at them both bubbling under water for a few seconds, then carried on towards the shore.

Once there, she carefully checked the shoreline for any signs of life, be it people or dog, and then stepped out of the water. For the life of her she couldn't see the hut! *I know it's here!* She walked forth and then back, right when the boys were coming out of the water.

"SHHH," she silently motioned to them by placing her index finger to her lips. For once, the boys obeyed and they joined her in the forth and back, back and forth, along the shoreline.

"There's nothing here," Howard finally whispered. "There's no Creepymère in these creepy woods,"

"Howard," Norma Jean said, "if you weren't such a meathead, I'd tell you that you almost said something poetic, however, because your head is made of hamburger, I'll resist."

Once again, Gyp snorted. Norma Jean and Howard looked at him and at each other. They were enjoying making this kid, with no siblings, laugh.

They sat down on some lake-water-choked poplar tree logs. Norma Jean looked toward the trees. They were just on the threshold of becoming a very thick forest. She sighed.

"Hey, Boss," Howard said, "can I go back and get the lunch?"

Norma Jean was ready to concede when something caught her eye. She stood up and walked towards a poplar tree.

"What do you see, Norma Jean," Gyp asked, joining her.

"I'm not sure," she said, "but look at this..." She pointed to a fleck of colour, blue colour, that was on the tree, just above their heads. "Why do you think someone painted this tree blue?" she asked no one in particular. "This is very odd..."

"Oh shoot," Howard groaned, "So, it's NOT lunch time after all?"

Ignoring him, Norma Jean said, "I just think this is odd..."

She walked around the tree and Gyp did the same. Howard eventually joined them. Norma Jean stopped at the blue fleck and put her hand on it, her back to the lake. She leaned forward to inspect it more closely. Gyp stopped right behind her, and Howard behind him. They stood in a straight line for a few minutes, each absorbing the details surrounding them.

Then abruptly, Howard pointed overtop both Gyp and Norma Jean's heads and said, "Look!"

"What?" both Gyp and Norma Jean said at the same time.

"There," he pointed again as he started to walk towards another tree that was just behind and a little to the left of the first one. "There's another blue bit of paint on that tree there!"

The others followed Howard. It was the same colour blue paint but the shape of the spot was different.

"Now, no one can tell me this isn't odd," Norma Jean said. They all stood in front of the tree for a few moments, looking up, down, left, right... nothing. No hut.

"Oh, my goodness, my goodness!" Norma Jean started low and slow and her pitch and tone raised with each word. "Oh my goodness!" she finally exalted. "I have an idea! I think I saw something in that book we got from the library last winter about the Indian totem poles."

Both Gyp and Howard looked at her and said, "Totem poles?"

"Yes!" Norma Jean ran back to the first tree. "Come here, you guys!" They obeyed. "I believe there's a kind of secret code here. I'm not exactly sure what to call it, but it's like a nature-lock. We can't find the hut because it's so well camouflaged. But the great-great-grand-mère wanted SOMEONE to find it, so she's created a back door."

"I'm pretty sure she wasn't thinking about us," Howard said.

"Here's what we have to do," Norma Jean continued, "Keep your eye on this first blue mark, then line up the next mark with your eye...you might need to move just a little..." she suited her action to her words, "...then look for another mark on a tree that lines up behind that second one..." Norma Jean adjusted her spot. Behind her Gyp and Howard did the same.

"I can't see anything with you in front of me, Norma Jean," Gyp said. "I'll go explore the trees that are behind that second blue-marked tree."

"Okay," Norma Jean said absently. She moved her body left and right, up and down, backing up to the lake shoreline as she did so. "Oh, please, please let this be what it is..." she whispered. *Oh sheesh; I'll be talking to St. Afan soon.*

"Hey, Mr. Giraffe, can you see anything?" Gyp called to Howard.

Norma Jean smiled to herself. *Really, for an only child, he's figured out this sibling language pretty quickly.*

Howard stretched his body upward and said, "Nope. And if I can't see it then it ain't here...wait...hey, Gyp go a little to your left...and now go back one tree...and look up...like at about my eye-level, you know, more normal for a twelve-year old..." he laughed. "Do you see anything? Is that...yellow?"

Gyp followed Howard's instructions. "It appears that being a monster child benefits you after all! Yes! This is yellow paint!" Both Norma Jean and Howard ran toward the tree.

"No, Howard," Norma Jean called to him.

"I'm not Nicky, for Pete's sake, Norma Jean," Howard protested.

"Just stay there and see if you can see anymore! And back up so you can get perspective."

"*Perspective?*" he muttered. "I have no idea what you're talking about." Nevertheless, he returned to his spot, backing up so that he could see a wider area, and commenced searching the trees in front of him.

After several moments he said, "THERE! Another yellow spot!" He pointed. "No, not there...you're cold...getting hotter...hotter...HOT! THERE! Can't you see it?"

Norma Jean and Gyp walked around the tree for several seconds and then Gyp shouted, "THERE!" and pointed to a yellow splash on the tree.

"SHHH!" Norma Jean said, but she was smiling. "Keep looking, Howard!"

Howard spent the next several moments peering into the woods, mumbling to himself about lunch.

"Keep looking, Howard!" Norma Jean encouraged, again.

"I am! I am!" he hissed back. "Good dog!" he muttered, just loud enough for Gyp to hear him. Several moments later he said, "I think I got it! Come back here, I'll show you!"

Norma Jean and Gyp ran back to the first tree and stood in front of Howard. "Okay," he said, "Do exactly what I tell you to. Exactly. Don't do anything..."

"I got it, Howard, you nitwit. I'll do EXACTLY what you tell me to," and then added in a whisper, "This once."

"I heard that, Norma Jean," Howard said.

Gyp elbowed them both. "Go on, Howard. You're making me crazy with suspense."

Howard physically moved Gyp and Norma Jean to the right spot and then said, "There."

"Where?" Norma Jean asked, exasperated.

"Just move your head ever so slightly, Norma Jean. Maybe back up a little to get *perspective*," Howard said. "It's so simple. I can't believe you can't see it..."

"Oh, DO shut up. I can't think..."

Much to his delight, for the next three minutes he explained and pointed. Finally, Gyp yelled, "I SEE IT! I SEE IT! You were RIGHT, Norma Jean!"

"SHE was right?!" Howard looked at Gyp, wide-eyed.

"About the clue, silly!" Gyp slapped Howard on the back. "And Howie found it, you ol' sharp-eyed coondog, you!"

Norma Jean was frantic to find the clue to open the backdoor. "Help me! Help me see it," she cried.

"It's the Acadian insignia! Look for that," Gyp stood in front of Norma Jean, willing her to find it.

"Oh yeah! It sure 'nough is!" Howard said, "I can see it clear as day, Norma Jean. Why can't you?"

"Be quiet, Howard! I can't think with all your yabbering!" Norma Jean said.

Howard and Gyp looked at each other and smiled.

"Yabber?" Howard repeated.

"Yes, yabber," Norma Jean said, impatiently.

"Cool word!" Gyp said, smiling.

Norma Jean knew that the innocent marking on one tree meant nothing to the casual observer—just a bit of blue paint splashed on a tree—but when several of those markings were seen from a certain *perspective* they became a picture. She moved her head, ever so slightly to the right, and screamed, "I GOT IT! I GOT IT!! I WAS RIGHT!! IT IS A CODE!! WE'VE JUST FOUND THE SECRET BACK DOOR TO THE HUT!"

And then the coondog started to howl.

"RUN!" Norma Jean said.

They all splashed back into the water and were untying the Western Red Cedar before you could say, *L'union fait la force*! Howard and Gyp secured the oars back into the locks and hurried that boat back to the middle of the lake. Once there, they all flopped down into the bottom, leaned against the seats and looked at one another. Slowly, Gyp started to laugh...Howard was about two snorts behind him...and Norma Jean followed four hiccups later.

"Oh man, I'm ready for another swim," Norma Jean said.

"I'm ready for lunch!" Howard said as he dug into the basket and pulled out a wax paper package of peanut butter and jam sandwiches.

Norma Jean and Gyp dived off the boat into the green water and swam vigorously for five minutes.

N.J. Bennett

"Leave some food for us!" Gyp called to Howard when he saw him, muffin in hand, sitting on the bench watching them. Howard shoved the berry treat into his mouth and jumped into the water.

"Hey, you're supposed to wait an hour after you eat, before you swim, Howard!" Norma Jean called to him.

He ignored her as he dog-paddled around the boat. After another 15 minutes they all piled in the boat again and let the sun dry their browning skin. Norma Jean and Gyp ate the rest of the sandwiches and Howard ate all the muffins. The pickle jar was empty of water when they realized it was time to start rowing ashore. They could see a small gray smoke signal coming from the Nielsen beach. That was all they needed to know Mum was starting the briquets for hamburgers.

"Start rowing, boys," Norma Jean shouted, then laughed.

Knowing they didn't have any choice, the boys dug in, sad to leave this happy day behind.

All of a sudden, Norma Jean reached over the edge of the boat and slammed her hand into the water. "Oh my goodness, oh my goodness...!"

"There she goes," Howard drawled to Gyp.

Gyp looked at them both and laughed. "What is it, Norma Jean? We're ready to hear anything!"

"We are IDIOTS, all three of us! We're the three little pigs, not the three musketeers!"

"Well, maybe Howard is, but..."

Norma Jean interrupted him, "The KEY, you dolts! The KEY! You dreamed about that key, Bernard..."

"Bernard?!" Gyp interrupted.

"Yes, *Bernard*," Norma Jean emphasized his name, "you dreamed about that key because it was hidden in the letter you stole from the museum. AND you heard your Dad and Mum TALK about a key, AND they found a key..."

Norma Jean dug into the lunch basket and pulled out the notebook. She had written the simple letter from *Père* in the notebook. "Listen," she said.

> *My dear Marie,*
> *You are the order to my past;*
> *You are the joy of my present;*
> *You are the hope for my future.*
> *The key to future happiness is*
> *Remembering your past.*
> *If you do not, the key is not for you,*
> *but for another.*
> *Love, Père*

"We've just discovered ANOTHER key, the KEY TO A BACK DOOR!" Norma Jean's voice rang across the water.

"Be quiet, Norma Jean!" Gyp reached out to cover her mouth. "If this really means something, you don't have to tell the keeper of the hut!"

"Oh, shoot!" Norma Jean covered her own mouth. "Do you think she heard me?"

"Naw," Howard said, "If she's as old as an alligator washboard she can't hear anything anymore!"

Gyp laughed, and Norma Jean relaxed.

"I have no idea what, but..." she put pencil to paper, "but it means something. Now, what do we write down?"

They discussed the possibilities and settled on the following:

<u>Clue Number 12:</u> Great-great-grand-mère's hut is camouflaged by a nature-coded backdoor and we found the KEY.

Much later that evening, when they had dragged their exhausted bodies to bed, Gyp sat up suddenly and said, "I forgot to tell you about that big blackbird."

Howard answered him with a snore.

Norma Jean laughed, "Better save it until tomorrow, Louise."

Gyp lay back down, "Okay, Hitchcock."

Norma Jean thought for a moment, then burst out laughing, "Good one. Grade nine drama did that play last fall. The Birds. Yeah, that was most certainly a Hitchcock moment this morning. Thanks for helping me."

"Splendid," Gyp answered as Norma Jean heard him roll over.

She had wanted to stay awake just a little bit longer to think...but...it had been a splendid day.

Chapter 7
HITCHCOCK
AND OTHER STUFF MUM KNOWS

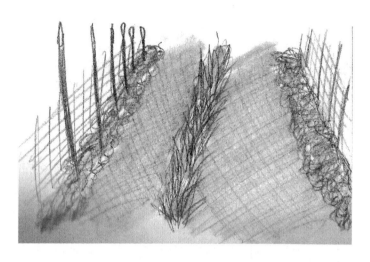

The next morning Norma Jean sent Gyp to the outhouse first. "Just go make sure Hitchcock hasn't returned," she said.

Both she and Howard followed at a distance. Sure enough, the big blackbird was perched on the corner of the outhouse roof.

Once again Gyp shouted, "*Laisse-la-tranquille!*" and "*Rentre chez toi!*" And once again, the blackbird lifted his corpulent body and flew away.

Norma Jean and Howard stepped closer and as they did so, Gyp knelt down and studied something on the worn grass in front of the outhouse.

"What is it?" Norma Jean asked, crouching beside him. Howard went into the outhouse and started whistling *You are my sunshine*. When he came back out, he squatted beside Norma Jean. They both looked at Gyp. "What is it?" Norma Jean repeated.

"It's time for breakfast at the big cabin and a little chat with your mom." Gyp stood, his black eyes roaming the sky, looking for Hitchcock.

"Sounds good to me!" Howard was already off at a run, Nicky close behind him. "I'll meet you there. I've got my swim trunks on! I'm ready for the day!"

Gyp went back into the small cabin and retrieved the French Bible in which he kept his mom's note and the stolen museum letter. When Norma Jean saw that, she grabbed the notebook. She found Gyp's somberness frighteningly exciting and was glad they were going to let Mum in on some of their secrets.

Norma Jean went into the closet and put her swimsuit on under her shorts and T-shirt, like she did every day at the lake. She sat on the steps to put on her runners, ran a brush quickly through her blonde hair, dashed to the outhouse, and joined Gyp, who was already halfway up the lane to the big cabin.

"So, what's going on?" she asked him.

"I'm not sure," he said. "I'd kinda like to talk it over with your mom...since mine's not here to talk to..." his voice trailed off.

"Good idea," Norma Jean said, glancing his way. "We can tell her any and everything, if you want."

"Maybe I will," he said.

Norma Jean got the distinct impression that there were many things she didn't know. She quickened her pace.

They had arrived at the cabin early enough to have breakfast with Dad and the boys before they all left for the farm. Mum was frying eggs and bacon and Kathy was browning toast, all on one massive wrought iron wood stove. There was toast in the warming oven and the three kids grabbed old china plates and loaded up. The three older brothers were seated on a pine bench on one long side of the roomy table. Allan and Les moved over and made room for Gyp between them.

"I wouldn't do it, if I were you," Norma Jean joked. "They'll think you're meat. You'll be a goner in seconds." If there was enough food, Mum always allowed the boys *seconds*...and there was ALWAYS enough food.

"Come on, Gypsy!" Les cajoled. "You're way too skinny for us to eat. Here, let me give you some bacon...fatten you up a bit. Then we'll be more interested." He laughed loud and the other boys joined in.

"Yeah, come on, Loui..." Norma Jean caught Gyp's nervous eyes and thought she'd better not tease him about being *Louise* in front of her big brothers. She was used to them and could take them on...all five at once if need be...but Gyp, well, he was an only child. This big-family business was new to him. She kept her mouth shut but smiled. If he needed rescuing, she'd be the first to step in.

She shoved in beside Dad. "How's my Yommpy-Doodle-Dandy?" he asked.

"Best ever," she said, holding out her plate for the egg Mum was handing her from a spatula. "Thanks for that new Western Red Cedar, Dad. It's totally cool!" She looked at Allan as she said *cool* and he laughed.

"Well," Dad said, "so glad I could provide some *cool* for the Nielsen family. Which reminds me," he looked at the boys, "No eight-tracks of those *Beatles* in my tractor, boys. Those long-hair *she loves you yeah yeah yeah* stuff. I don't approve. You'll find your eight-tracks thrown to the stubble if I find anymore of that nonsense." He looked at the boys who were very interested in their bacon.

"How do you know what the *Beatles* sound like, Dad?" Howard asked, not knowing that THIS was the time NOT to ask questions.

Dad looked at Mum, who smiled ever so slightly, then sighed, and said, "Okay, Allan, you take the Versatile tractor to the Pixley quarter and cultivate what Keith didn't get done last week before the rain. Les, you check all the teeth on the swather and change any broken ones. Keith, you fix the fence on the chicken coop, west side, you'll see it. There's chicken wire in the machine shed."

"Chickens?" all the kids said at once.

Dad looked at Mum. She smiled. "Yes, chickens," he said. "Your Mum has a hankering to go into private business."

"Again?" Keith said. "Do we HAVE to do chickens again?"

"Those were turkeys, last time, Keith," Mum said. "This time it's chickens."

"Oh," Keith mocked, "I see the difference."

The big boys started in on Keith as the lucky one who got to fix the chicken coop...sissy job. If he'd remembered to take the *Beatles* eight-track out of the tractor Dad wouldn't have picked him!

Dad continued, "And Howard and Norma Jean, you..." he smiled, "You probably want to ride along to the farm so you can get back into that garden and pick the peas..."

At the same time, Gyp yelled, "YES!" and Norma Jean and Howard yelled, "NO!"

Everyone laughed. "Mum?" Dad asked his wife. "Do you need the kids to go to the farm to work today?"

She looked at Norma Jean and Howard, "Yes. Sorry, kids. The garden simply needs to be tended."

"But, Mum, I've already got my swimsuit on," Norma Jean pleaded.

"Sorry, again, Norma Jean. But run down now and have one quick dip while Kathy and I get everything ready to go." Norma Jean jumped up.

"Wait a minute," Dad said. He got up and pulled an old worn Bible off the shelf behind him. "Let's listen to what God has to say to us today." He opened it and read, "*Better is one day in your courts than a thousand elsewhere; I would rather be a doorkeeper in the house of my God than dwell in the tents of the wicked. Psalms 84:10.*" He closed the book and looked at the boys. "Remember that, sons." They looked at him and nodded.

The family dispersed, going their separate ways, taking their dishes to the outdoor kitchen first. Mum had heated some water and Kathy was already washing up the breakfast pots and pans.

Baby Barry was in his highchair, happy to be eating for as long as he wanted. Norma Jean kissed him on his towheaded hair. "See you soon, Little Manny. I'm off for a swim. When we get to the farm, I'll let you come with me to the pea-patch."

An hour later they were loading up the 1962 green Chevy pickup. Norma Jean and Howard jumped into the back. "Come on, Gyp," Norma Jean called. "Since you're company, I'll give you the wheel well to sit on. Howard will give it to you on the way back, won't you Howard?"

"Sure!" Howard said. "It's all yours."

Norma Jean put an old farm jacket under her bum and sat down under the back window, facing the tailgate of the pickup. She reached up and knocked on the window behind her, knowing that Baby Barry would be standing there watching them. She could hear him laugh. Howard and Gyp both took a seat on opposite wheel wells and Mum started the engine.

"Hey, Mum!" Howard suddenly called, "Can I drive?"

Mum looked out the back window, shook her head, then turned to say something to Kathy. Kathy's passenger door flew open and she walked around the back of the truck. "Thanks for reminding me, Howard. If I'm going to get my Learner's License soon I'd better start driving more."

"Shoot," Howard said.

Mum slid across the seat and put Baby Barry on her lap. She turned to check on the kids in the back. "Hang on tight to the sides of the truck, Gyp!" she yelled.

Kathy lurched into first gear and Gyp went sliding off the forward-side of the wheel well. "Oh!" he said, "I see what you mean!"

Norma Jean and Howard laughed. "Hang on for dear life," Howard said, then yelled, "because KATHY IS DRIVING!"

Kathy looked in her rear mirror, grinned, and did her best to burn rubber. Gyp went flying off the wheel well again. "That one was meant for me!" Howard laughed. "Nice try, Kathy!" he yelled.

They drove down the winding, dirt laneway, past the small cabin, past the gooseberry bushes at the gate to the hayfield, and turned west onto the Pine Lake road. After Kathy had successfully found third gear they bumped along the gravel road for the next eight miles.

Gyp managed to stay in his precarious seat the whole time. Norma Jean looked at him: dust was swirling around him as the truck kicked up the loose gravel and dirt. His blackbird-black hair was getting long...*Dad's gonna include him in the next Saturday night kitchen barber shop*...his eyes squinted both because of sun and wind; he smiled the whole eight miles to the farm.

Kathy lurched down the farm laneway, changing from third, to second, to first gear.

"You shoulda let me drive, Mum!" Howard yelled.

Kathy slammed on the brakes and Howard went flying off the wheel well, banging his shoulder on the window where Baby Barry was peering out at him.

"Hey!" he yelled.

Norma Jean and Gyp laughed. Howard grinned.

Kathy pulled into the driveway, careful not to hit the foot-high rock wall that Mum had built the summer before. To the right of the truck was the living room window, and under it was a small flower bed, full of perennials: bleeding hearts, snap-dragons, fuchsias, and an ornamental cranberry bush. In front and to the left of the truck was the grassy yard, flanked on the north side by the lilac-bordered laneway and on the east and south by three rows of ash and poplar trees. The fire pit was in the south-east corner of the spacious yard.

The kids jumped out of the back of the truck. Mum opened her door and yelled, "One hour, kids! I'll honk the truck horn when it's time to meet me on the porch steps." And they were off.

"We haven't let Gyp pick his own climbing tree yet, Norma Jean!" Howard said as he led them to the rows of trees. "Come on!"

Norma Jean and Howard were quickly to the top of two different flourishing poplar trees. Four trees separated them.

"Come on, Gyp! Try some out and then pick one. If it's yours, no one else gets to climb it," Howard continued.

Gyp went from one tree to another...he touched the bark of each tree, looked at its leaves, pulled on its branches...and then started climbing.

"This is it, this is the one," he said.

Norma Jean and Howard looked at each other. They knew that Gyp had picked Keith's tree.

"That's the perfect tree," Norma Jean yelled back to him.

They also both knew that the boys were already beyond climbing trees. Gyp didn't need to know and it didn't matter.

They spent the next 20 minutes climbing up and down, up and down. Then Norma Jean said, "I need to go to our fort and get some stuff." And once again, they were off.

They could see Keith working on the chicken coop fence as they wandered past the stand-alone garage that was set 200 feet behind the farm house.

"Hey, Howard!" Keith yelled. "Bring me a pair of pliers from the garage, will ya?"

Howard and Gyp ducked into the garage to search the tool bench for pliers. Norma Jean kept on going to the fort. It was exactly as they had left it last week: four plywood walls, half a roof, apple crate shelf, cow bell at the entry. She went to the shelf and grabbed the county map. *Maybe this will help me discover the hut.* She stuck it in her cut-off jeans back pocket.

Keith had enlisted help from Howard and Gyp, so Norma Jean skirted the chicken yard and headed back to the house. She snuck past Mum who was already hanging laundry on the line and went to the bedroom that she and Kathy shared. She pulled out a few more hand-me-down T-shirts from her dresser drawer. Then she went to the inside porch and poked through all the shoes and boots to see if she could find one more pair of runners since she had used the pair she had at the lake as water shoes. She scored with a pair of black tie-ups that fit her perfectly. Putting all these things into a brown paper bag and then into the bed of the pickup, she headed back to the chicken yard to join the others. Just as Keith was about to enlist her help too, the pickup horn sounded.

"Oh, sorry, Keith," Norma Jean smiled. "Gotta go."

"Have fun working in the garden," Keith teased.

Norma Jean's heart sank. She'd rather work on the chicken coop. ANYTHING on the farm besides the garden. She loved everything about the farm...except the garden. It was just TOO big. The northeast corner of the farmyard was ALL garden. Row upon row of potatoes, then two LONG rows of raspberries, then several LONG rows each of peas, carrots, turnips, cabbage, parsnips, onions. Mum had even tried to grow broccoli and brussels sprouts. There were gooseberry and currant bushes to pick and then can for winter eating. She just hated it. There simply was no other word to describe it.

They met Mum on the cement porch and she handed Norma Jean a brown paper bag, Howard a Roger's syrup can and belt, and Gyp...nothing.

"Norma Jean," she said, "Peas. Howard...raspberries. And Gyp weed the turnip and cabbage rows."

Howard went behind the huge lilac bush that almost covered the kitchen window, turned on the hose, and followed it to its end where he took a drink of gushing well-water. Gyp and Norma Jean did the same. Then Howard filled Nicky's water bowl. Nicky had come to the farm with Dad and the boys earlier and had just now careened down the machine shed hill to join the three younger kids. There was a flurry of tail-wagging, and barking.

"Hey, ol' boy," Howard said, spraying him with the hose. "You can't wait to work in the garden, can you. Here...take my bucket...go on, take it!"

Nicky ran circles around all of them, barking recklessly.

"Quiet, Nicky." Mum finally said, "You'll wake Barry."

Nicky obeyed and sat down beside Mum, panting and dripping water from his jowls.

"Off you go, kids!" Mum said and went back to the clothes line.

"Wait, what's Kathy doing"? Norma Jean grumbled.

"None of your business," Mum didn't even turn to look at Norma Jean.

"It's not fair. She LIKES the garden. Why doesn't she have to do this?" Again, Mum ignored her.

"Oh come on, crabby-pants," Gyp said. "Let's just go get it done."

"*Laissez les bons temps rouler!*" Howard shouted and strapped the syrup bucket around his waist.

"Oh be quiet, Howard," Norma Jean muttered.

An hour later, Mum, with Baby Barry on her hip, and Kathy, joined them. Mum put Barry down beside Norma Jean, in the middle of the pea patch. He immediately got up and toddled toward her open bag of picked peas. "Hey, pick your own peas, Little Manny," she laughed.

Mum and Kathy joined Howard in the raspberry patch. "Gyp, you can move to the carrot rows whenever you want," Mum called.

"*Bon!*" Gyp called back.

Looking around her, Norma Jean realized this was an excellent time to get Gyp talking. Mum was here...Kathy was also here but Norma Jean didn't think it would matter. She never paid too much attention to them.

"So, Gyp, tell us about..." Norma Jean wasn't sure where to start. "Um...tell us about..."

"Hitchcock!" Howard squawked as he said it.

"Yeah," Norma Jean chimed in, "Hitchcock."

Mum looked at them.

"Don't worry, Mum...we're talking about a blackbird," Norma Jean said.

"Go on, then, Gyp. Let's hear all about Hitchcock," Mum said.

"You start, Norma Jean," Gyp coaxed. "It started with you."

"Well, the other day when I went to the outhouse there was a big blackbird...thus the name Hitchcock..."

"*Thus*," Howard gibed. "Listen to her."

Norma Jean ignored him and continued: "The stupid bird wouldn't let me in! Squawked and fussed and scared the livin' day-lights out of me. Then Gyp comes out and says..."

"*Rentre chez toi!*" Gyp bellowed, "and *Laisse-la-tranquille!*"

"And the beastly thing flies away," Norma Jean said. "So, what did you say, Gyp?"

"I said, *Go back home!* and *Leave her alone!*" he replied.

Norma Jean stopped picking peas and looked at him, "Why?" she asked.

Gyp looked at Mum, she nodded. "Because I think the great-great-grand-mère sent that blackbird as a warning to us."

"Ha! Ha!" Howard laughed. "That's a good one!"

No one else joined his laughter. "What?" he said, "you don't think that's funny?"

"It would be if we weren't Cajun," Gyp said. "You see, in our culture we're very superstitious and that blackbird is an omen."

"How do you know?" Howard asked. "We got plenty of Hitchcock's here in Alberta."

"I wasn't sure until I saw another omen on the ground in front of the outhouse this morning," Gyp said.

"It was just a pile of...stuff...like broom straws, for Pete's sake," Howard said.

"HOWARD!" Norma Jean hollered. "LET THE GUY TALK!"

"Sheesh, I just think it's dumb, that's all," he mumbled.

"I don't expect you to understand it, Howard," Gyp said, "but I think your mom might."

Mum nodded her head. "What did you find this morning, Gyp?" she asked.

"I found 13 broomstick straws...you were right, Howard, laying side by side, in a nicely cleared out circle, right in front of the outhouse, the very place the blackbird had showed up."

"That's very unusual," Mum said.

"Why...?" Howard started.

"HOWARD!" Norma Jean yelled again. "Eat some raspberries!"

"But you always like it when I ask *why*,"

Howard said.

"Yes, but NOT NOW!" She threw a clump of dirt in his direction. "Keep going Gyp..."

"Well, it's just odd because it's two opposite omens, "Gyp said. "Would you agree..." he hesitated, "Auntie?"

"Calling me 'Auntie' is perfect, Gyp. And maybe...maybe they were opposite, but not necessarily."

"What do you mean, Mum?" Norma Jean kept working, lifting up the heavy-laden pea vines, plucking them, and throwing them into the brown paper bag. Baby Barry had found a muddy spot in the rich, black soil and was practically purring with pleasure.

"Are you ready for a story?" Mum said.

"YES!" they all shouted, except Kathy— but even she turned around to look at Mum.

"There have been stories in our family about buried treasure..."

Howard couldn't help himself, "BURIED TREASURE!!!"

And Norma Jean couldn't stop herself, "If you interrupt ONE MORE TIME you'll have to sleep in the outhouse tonight!"

"Like to see you make me," he muttered. Nevertheless, he kept his mouth shut for the rest of the story.

Norma Jean took out the notebook, and silently wrote:

<u>Clue Number 13:</u> Omens…more later.

Chapter 8
A *TRÈS BON* STORY FULL OF *GRIS-GRIS*

Mum continued picking raspberries while she talked:

"The Cajun people have always been very superstitious. When *Le Grand Dérangement* happened in 1755, families had to flee, leaving most everything behind. Many treasures were buried at the last hour and remain buried to this day.

"When a blackbird—Hitchcock—appears, that *could* be an omen. You see, Cajun treasure is guarded by ghosts, and omens may appear in the form of blackbirds, cows, or even the moon. So, MAYBE Hitchcock was an omen sent to either warn or encourage our family regarding the treasure. And MAYBE the 13 broomstick straws were also an omen to protect us against the Cajun garou—werewolf. I know all this gris-gris—*o m e n s*—stuff sounds ridiculous to talk about standing here in central Alberta, in the middle of a big farm garden; nevertheless, this is my family's history. We are Cajun people, full of stories, many of which I've learned since contacting Gyp's mum and dad.

"But back to the present story...the 13 broomstick straws are laid down in front of a door to protect the family from the garou. Now, why they were laid in front of the outhouse is a question I'll leave to the great-great-grand-mère—not that I know *for sure* that it was her, but I have my suspicions. As I said, the broomstick straws are for our protection...The werewolf can't count higher than 12, so when it gets to the 13th straw it is so confused it has to start again, and again, and again, until dawn when it must flee the sun. It's really just a bunch of silliness and Dad doesn't like me to talk about it, nevertheless, it is my family history. And Gyp's. I've been a little more interested in it since I've been corresponding with his parents."

She paused and looked at Howard. "And NOW, I will take any questions,"

They were all silent for a few moments.

"Cool!" Howard finally said, "But really, really weird."

"Has our family treasure ever been found, Mum? And why have we never heard about this before?" Norma Jean asked.

"No, our family has never found treasure. I'm not sure there is any. And I don't speak of it because it's not really part of mine and your dad's life together. We're kinda busy with a few other things," she laughed. "Besides, maybe the family treasure IS the French Bible and ancient letter from *Père*."

"Maybe..." Norma Jean said. She could see that Dad wouldn't be too crazy about this stuff.

"I can give you a little more history, if you want," Mum said. "It's a bit of a long story."

"Well, as you can see," Norma Jean said, "We have plenty of time!" She motioned with her arm to the vast garden. "Unless, that is, we're finished already!" she looked at Mum eagerly.

"How many bags of peas do you have, Norma Jean?" Mum asked.

"Two...full," she replied.

"And Howard? Did you pick that whole west row of raspberries?" she continued.

"Yup, I have a very full bucket, too." Howard answered.

"And Gyp, how's the turnips?"

"*Très bon*," he said.

"Okay then. We can take the peas to the lake because Bedstefar and Bedstemor are going to join us this afternoon, and you know how she loves to shell peas!"

"Thank goodness!" Norma Jean said. The last thing she wanted to do was sit on the porch steps and shell peas the rest of the afternoon. "So, Mum, do all the Dupre families think that the letter is the treasure?" Norma Jean asked.

"Norma Jean, did you REALLY just ask Mum if we could stay in the garden longer," Howard teased.

"Never mind, Howard," Mum said. She came out from the raspberry bushes, handed her bucket to Kathy, and picked up a very dirty baby Barry.

They all started walking toward the porch and the garden hose. After they had washed up and Mum had put Barry in the baby seat of the steel swing Dad had made, they sat on the porch steps, drinking water. Kathy had taken the clothes off the line and had sat down on the steps to fold them.

Mum began, "In 1680 an Acadian family settled along the Bay of Fundy in a village they named *Grand Pre*. As more families joined them they cleared the land to farm..."

"Like our farm?" Howard asked.

"There was wheat and barley, like we have, but they also planted peas," Mum said.

"No! A whole farm of peas!!" Norma Jean threw herself off the porch step and lay prostrate on the grass, groaning.

"And who's interrupting now?" Howard said.

"ANYWAY," Mum continued, "They farmed PEAS, flax, and planted gardens of cabbages and pumpkins, and orchards of apples and plums, and they raised cattle and sheep.

"Eventually, they added wharfs along the shoreline and soldiers from the garrisons at Annapolis Royal and Louisburg came to purchase supplies. They would pay for the goods using gold. And the piggy bank of choice for these Acadian farmers was an iron kettle, and the vault of choice was the deep-dark dirt."

"It was called *Acadian gold*, wasn't it, Auntie?" Gyp asked.

"Right you are, Gyp. Acadian gold. And the people amassed huge amounts of it, as there was no Kressges to go shopping at.

"There was much unrest as the British vied for power with the French and the Mi'kmaq. The Acadians had tried to remain a neutral people, but neither the French nor the British trusted them to not side with one or the other. So, on September 5, 1755, the British came to town and asked all the Acadian men and boys to come to a meeting at the church at *Grand Pre*, to discuss the future. Once there, they locked the doors. And this is how *Le Grand Dérangement* began. The people were deported and sent to places unknown—such as Louisiana."

"Which is why our family lives there," Gyp said.

"Yes, it is," Mum confirmed. "But, before the people fled they HID their treasures. Much of the gold was already buried, but they added to it as quickly as they could. The people were loaded up onto ships and watched their homes burn as they set sail. The British then gave their land to New England settlers, and with it, buried kettles of Acadian gold."

"You mean there's STILL gold buried in Nova Scotia?" Howard asked.

"Absolutely," Mum said.

"Cool!" Howard joined Norma Jean on the grass and said, "Nova Scotia, here we come!"

Mum laughed and said, "Sure, right after the peas are picked, the raspberries canned, the potatoes dug, the carrots topped, the..."

"I get it! I get it!" Howard flopped back on the grass. "It's still a cool story; at least the part of buried Acadian gold."

Mum looked at her watch, "And now, it's dinner time. Would you watch Barry, Norma Jean?"

"Sure thing," she said, giving him another push on the swing.

Mum went into the house. Kathy had already gone in several minutes earlier to put the potatoes on.

Howard and Gyp came over and got on either end of the teeter-totter. "This is all very..." Norma Jean started.

"Don't say it," Howard interrupted.

"ODD!" Gyp laughed.

"Well, that, AND splendidly exciting," Norma Jean said. "Hmm...I need to think. You two be quiet for a minute."

Gyp and Howard looked at each other and immediately began to push the teeter-tooter to its limits. Howard's heavier body made the fulcrum unequal, so he moved towards the center. This kept him from landing too hard and kept the force of gravity even. Up and down they went while Norma

Jean pushed baby Barry and thought, and thought...
I've seen something somewhere...

Les, Keith, and Dad arrived from different points of the farmyard, and went inside the house to have dinner. Mum had put a roast in the oven as soon as she got there from the lake and it was ready. Howard and Gyp joined them. Still, Norma Jean continued to push Barry.

Finally, Mum came out to the porch and said, "Norma Jean, what are you doing? I can hear Barry crying all the way from the dining room!"

"Oh!" Norma Jean stopped Barry's swing, "I'm so sorry Little Manny. Here, let's go get you some roast beef." She lifted him out and Mum came down the steps to get him. "Mum, can I take my roast beef in a sandwich to the lake to eat later?" she asked.

"Yes," Mum said, "But I also need you to walk up to the Pixley quarter with Allan's dinner. Would you do that for me, please? Dad doesn't want him to stop cultivating. I'll include your sandwich too, just in case you change your mind."

"Okay," she said.

Ten minutes later she was walking up the south road and then she cut east across the cultivated furrows towards the dusty spot where she could see the tractor. She was carrying the hot food in a cardboard box, and had a small knapsack across her shoulders.

Allan saw her coming and stopped the big tractor, opened the door of the cab and smiled. "Now, that's exactly what I was hoping to see! Dinner!"

She handed him the box, taking her own dinner sandwich out first.

"Wanna ride for a while, Norma Jean?" he asked.

"Sure!" she said, "I want to ride as far as the sand dunes. Can you let me off there?"

"Hey! I'll take the person who brings me dinner wherever they want!" Allan sat on the top steps and quickly ate his roast beef, potatoes, gravy, and carrots, talking the whole time about the new motor boat he had seen on the lake last week.

Norma Jean listened absently while checking for Indian arrowheads in the deep furrows that had just been plowed. "Uh-huh" she said every now and then.

"Well, I can see you're really interested," Allan laughed. "Doesn't matter. Jump in!"

He threw the box of dirty dishes behind the big leather seat.

Norma Jean climbed up the stairs with one hand, and held onto the foil package that carried her sandwich with the other hand. She sat on the left armrest of the driver's chair and shut the door of the cab.

Allan reached down and pushed the eight-track back in. The *Beatles* blared loud and clear. *We all live in a yellow submarine*. He looked at her and grinned. She grinned back. He knew his secret was safe with her.

They bumped along the field until they came to the east road ditch. Norma Jean jumped down, waving her thanks. He waved back and turned the big Versatile around to plow the next row.

The sand dunes weren't really *sand dunes*, but they called them that anyway. The ditch had a nice sandy bank on which a kid could pretend to snow ski in the summer. Norma Jean wasn't interested in playing right now, however. Instead she followed along the creek that bordered the Pixley quarter and the neighbour's land. Minutes later she crawled into a secret alcove that she had crafted out of pussy willow branches and rocks. Not even Howard knew about it.

Sometimes a girl just needed to be alone. To think. And think she did. *Now, where, oh where did I see*...she took off her knapsack and put her lunch in it. Eating was not compatible with thinking. Instead, she pulled out the notebook, opened it and reread the clues. *I'm missing something. I can feel it.* She chewed her pencil. *What is it about that French Bible ...no, it's not the Bible...it's something else...*She thought, and thought, and thought but it just wouldn't come to her.

Half an hour later, she ran the quarter mile back to the farmhouse, frustrated and empty headed as far as clues were concerned.

As she walked down the laneway, she could see Dad and Mum standing beside the pickup. They were talking intently and didn't notice her as she walked behind them and up the sidewalk towards the house.

She hadn't meant to eavesdrop but...she turned on the hose and got a long drink of water. The sound of running water made Dad turn and he and Mum stopped talking.

He turned back to Mum and said, "Do whatever you think is right, Florence," and kissed her. He waved to Norma Jean and said, "See you at suppertime! Go have a swim for me, Norma Jean!" And he was off to the machine shed where the combine awaited his inspection.

Mum reached into the truck window and honked the horn loud and long. "What took so long, Norma Jean? We're ready to go back to the lake!" she called.

"Sorry, Mum! I'm ready too!" She jumped in the bed of the truck just as Howard, Gyp, and Nicky came running from behind the barn, and Kathy and Barry came out of the house.

"Let's go, everyone!" Mum called. She jumped in the driver's seat, changed her mind and slid over. Kathy smiled, handed Barry to Mum and got behind the steering wheel.

"Oh no!" Howard moaned. "Not again! I'm not gonna be able to ski cause this shoulder hurts so bad; in fact I could barely pick raspberries because of the Kathy-bruise that's coming on my head; and..."

Kathy roared the engine to life, put pedal to the metal as she slammed the truck into reverse, sending all the kids flying. Sometimes, she surprised everyone. Even Mum.

"Howard, you don't need to give me the wheel well," Gyp laughed. "YOU take it!" he plopped down on the denim farm coat underneath the back window and Norma Jean and Howard took their places on either wheel well.

"HIT IT!" Howard shouted. And Kathy booked it to the lake.

By four o'clock they had flippers on and were swimming contentedly in the murky lake water, checking every so often for blood suckers.

And still Norma Jean thought...

That night, while the Coleman lantern played havoc with the shadows, the three kids sat on their own beds and talked. Norma Jean had the notebook in front of her.

"All right," she said, "It's time to decide what's a clue and what isn't. Howard, what do you think?" Norma Jean looked at him.

"I think...I think that the letter might NOT be the treasure...and that COULD mean there's treasure. I mean real treasure, like GOLD, somewhere."

"I agree," Norma Jean said, and wrote:

Clue Number 14: Our families both have a historical riddle that had originally been given to *Marie* from *Père*. They had been stuffed into a 1730's French Bible. It alludes to treasure. What IS the treasure? Could it be Acadian gold?"

"You don't know if it was *stuffed,* Norma Jean," Howard said.

"Doesn't matter," she said. "I think it was *stuffed.*"

Howard rolled his eyes.

"I can still see you, Howard," Norma Jean said.

He laughed, "Okay...but all*ude*?"

"Gyp?" Norma Jean said, ignoring him, "Anything?"

"Of course! The broomstick straws," he said, "And the fact that your mom thinks the great-great-grand-mère did it."

"Exactly," Norma Jean said as she wrote:

<u>Clue Number 15:</u> The great-great-grand- mère (at least Mum thinks it was her) sent us an omen...

"Should we include Hitchcock?" Norma Jean asked them.

"Oh, yeah," said Howard. "Gotta have the bird in there. Say: the creepymère sent us TWO omens.

"That's not very respectful, Howard," Norma Jean said.

He ignored her, and she corrected the clue:

<u>Clue Number 15:</u> The great-great-grand-mère sent us TWO omens: Hitchcock and the broomstick straws.

She read them aloud, then said, "I know there's something else but I just can't put my finger on it..."

"It'll come, Norma Jean," Gyp said as he lay down. "Just stop thinking about it and it'll come. Who's turning off the lantern?"

Howard was already snoring.

"I guess that'll be me," Norma Jean said as she put her bare feet on the cold wood floor and walked over to the table.

The wood stove was still warm and cracks of light escaped from the heavy cast iron burner lids. The ornate oven door looked like a blackbird...at least in the shadowy tricks both the light and her mind were playing.

She put the notebook on the table and said, "Goodnight, Gyp."

And as usual, she was the only one still awake.

Chapter 9
A SUDDEN TRIP IS PLANNED

It was Saturday evening. The whole family was back at the farmhouse, preparing for Sunday. The boys worked until 8PM, then walked onto the porch, shed their dirty coveralls, which Mum put directly into the washing machine, bathed, and got in the lineup for haircuts.

"Hey, Dad," Les said, "I don't need a haircut this week."

Dad glanced over at his second oldest son but didn't say anything. Keith, who was currently the one under the razor said, "Oh yes you do, dude. If I do, you do."

"No, really, I don't," Les continued. He walked into the living room, waiting to be called for pancakes.

Norma Jean could see Dad glance over at Mum. She smiled and shrugged her shoulders.

"Hey!" Keith protested, "Ya mean we had an option?!"

Again, Dad kept quiet. Norma Jean could see a slight twitch on the right side of his lip. She loved watching her family. Pretending to be polishing the church shoes, she watched and listened as Keith said, "Okay, this is it. This is the very last haircut I'm getting until...until...I get married!"

"Oh, ya like her, do ya?" Norma Jean quipped. She'd noticed the steady stream of girls that visited the lake all summer. Sometimes one was there more often than the others, and Keith had ONE that had been there a lot this summer. Used to being ignored by them, she kept polishing shoes.

"Your turn, Howard," Dad said, taking the cape off Keith and walking out to the porch to shake it off.

"I don't think I need a haircut this week," Howard said.

Dad looked at him, Howard sighed and got up on the kitchen stool. The electric razor began—from the neck up to the middle of the back of his head, Howard got razored, then scissored on the top.

"Gyp?" Dad looked across the kitchen to the black-haired boy who had been sitting at the table, silently watching. "You need a haircut? I'm pretty good at it. Just look at these boys! Well, don't look at Les, he needs a haircut, but look around at the rest. I bet you've never seen anything like it. Regular Barber-shop right here at the Nielsen farm every Saturday night, whether you need it or not."

Mum laughed.

"Umm," Gyp stammered, "Sure! I guess..."

Dad shook out the cape again and revved up the razor. "Don't worry, Son," Dad said, "I usually leave part of the head."

Norma Jean laughed. Gyp was getting used to them and he jumped up on the stool. "I'd like it to be a little long on the sides..."

Dad laughed. "Son, you've been mistaken...I only have ONE haircut...that's the one you'll get,"

"Oh," Gyp said and looked at Howard's nearly shaved head. "Okay," he said hesitantly.

"You can go join the long-hair in the living room if you want," Dad said, holding the razor inches away from the back of Gyp's head. What's your decision?"

"Wait a minute!" Keith yelled from the living room where he, Les, and Allan had opened up a game of Monopoly. "Why does HE get a choice?"

"Good thing I cut that boy's hair, Mum," he winked at his wife. "He's on the verge of becoming one of those long-haired good-for-nothings that sing..."

Norma Jean interrupted him and belted out, "*She loves you yeah, yeah, yeah*..."

"All right, Yommpy-Doodle-Dandy, we might have to talk about where you heard that song," he glanced over to his youngest daughter and raised his eyebrows.

Norma Jean could see Allan, in the living room, staring at her with the threat of tar and chicken feathers written deep into his blue eyes.

"Dad," Norma Jean said, "You'd have to be DEAD to not hear the Beatles now and then. She looked at Allan and he sat back down and bought Park Place.

"Well, Florence," he said, "I guess that does it. We've been invaded and here I am, alive and well to hear it." He sighed and Gyp got an especially short haircut.

Dad cleaned up the barber shop and Mum set up the beauty salon. "Hop up, Norma Jean, it's curler time." There was no complaining from Norma Jean; she liked having the pink foam rollers put in once a week; that is, she liked the effect from them when she went to church but sleeping on them was a different story. Mum curled Kathy's hair too and then she turned to the pancake batter that was sitting on the counter, ready for the sizzling griddle that Dad had started the bacon on.

Saturday night at the Nielsen farm: baths, haircuts, curlers, shoe polish, pancakes, bacon, eggs, saskatoon syrup.

They sat around the humongous dining room table and talked about the week behind them and the week ahead of them.

"Boys," Dad started, "I need you to hay the lake property this week. May as well start it on

Monday. The kids can help you," He looked at Norma Jean and Howard, "That sound good, kids?"

"Sure," they both said. They loved being in the fields, and especially at the lake where the water called their names several times a day...and everyone listened. Fields and gardens were two VERY different things.

"Can we shoot gophers after we hay?" Les asked Dad.

"Yeah, that'd be fine," Dad said, forking himself another thick slice of bacon, "Just watch out for Nicky. And that dog from Spruce Bay's been..."

"That's a Catahoula Leopard, Dad," Howard interrupted.

"What?" Keith said.

"Keith, don't say *what*," Mum corrected.

"*Pardon?*" Keith repeated.

"That's a coondog, of course! Anybody knows that," Howard swaggered. "Isn't it, Mum?" he looked at her.

"As a matter of fact, it is a Catahoula Leopard...a coondog," Mum agreed.

"Mum," Les chided, "How do you know that?"

Mum looked at Dad. He nodded and she continued, "We have family from down there where coondogs come from: Louisiana. Where Gyp's family is from. You all know he's distantly related..."

"Yeah, but *distantly*, right?" Les asked.

"Yes, distantly," Norma Jean cut in, "But still *related*!" she looked at Gyp, hoping he wasn't bothered by Les' smart aleck comment.

"Anyway," Dad said, "Just be careful and watch for Nicky and that coondog."

"And the kids!" Mum added.

"Why's that coondog there, anyway?" Les couldn't let it drop.

Mum looked at the three kids that were sitting on the piano bench at the end of the table. "Dogs wander, Les. They just do. Even Nicky does," she said.

"Well, that coondog has never wandered before. Serve him right if he got some buckshot in his behind," Les held up his knife and pretended it was his shotgun. "Bang!" he shouted.

Barry started to laugh and the subject was changed.

Dad reminded them all to wear life jackets when they waterskied, and for the boys to be careful with all their...shenanigans. The truth of it was, and everyone knew it, Dad loved shenanigans as much as his boys did.

"Hey, Dad," Allan said. "We've been thinkin' up this way to get pulled behind the boat on a piece of plywood..."

Keith broke in, "It's so cool! We're gonna cut a board into a perfect four foot round circle, paint it, and see if we can *ski* on it."

They all looked at Dad.

122

"And when are we going to try out this new cool toy out?" he asked

The boys looked at each other.

"Well," Les continued, "We've already made it, actually. We're ready to go!"

"All right then," Dad said, "Right after church tomorrow. Let's see if you can make this thing work."

The boys looked at each other and smiled.

"Oh, and by the way, kids," Dad said, "I stopped in at the boat supply store yesterday and somehow came home with a new pair of junior-skis. Don't know how that happened, but there you go! It happened."

"COOL!" Howard shouted, "But I want to try that board too, boys!"

"You can, Howard," Allan said, "But I was thinking of seeing if I could ski with you on my shoulders. Wanna try it?"

"YES!" Howard shouted again.

"Me too!" Norma Jean joined in.

"I still wanna try that board!" Howard said.

"You'll have to wait your turn, kid," Les patted his head.

"Stop it, Les," Howard pushed his hand away. He hated being treated like a child.

"All right, kids," Dad said. "Everyone gets their turn. And Howard, you can always help me drive the boat."

"Me too!" Norma Jean shouted.

"Me too!' Gyp joined her.

Everyone looked at him, and he pulled his shoulders in and put his head down. Then everyone started laughing. Baby Barry, sitting in the highchair at the corner of the table between Dad and Mum, banged his spoon, and saskatoon syrup splashed all over Dad's face.

"Hey, hey, hey! Settle down there, Little Manny!" Dad said.

"Gyp goes first on the new junior-skis," Les said, and everyone agreed, even Howard.

Gyp beamed. It made Norma Jean happy to see how much he liked her family. Every now and then, however, she caught him with that bright gleam in his eye—tears are pretty hard to stop or to hide. She wished he'd just let them flow when he was around her and Howard. *Maybe he will, someday.*

Kathy and Mum had gone in the kitchen to parboil the fresh peaches that Bedstefar and Bedstemor had just brought from the Okanogan. Kathy was peeling the plump, sweet fruit, and Mum was cutting it into fruit bowls, ready for fresh, cold cream to be poured on top.

"Hang on, Barry. Dessert's coming," Dad said as he wiped his face, then reached over to do the same for Barry.

"I'll help you, Dad," Norma Jean said and went into the washroom to get a clean rag. She came back and started cleaning up the syrup that was everywhere.

The phone rang: two long rings, and one short. Dad looked at Mum. She put the knife down, quickly washed her hands at the kitchen sink, dried them on her apron and went to answer it.

There were six farms that shared the same phone line, each with a different ring. When the Nielsen phone rang it was usually Bedstefar or Bedstemor. However, there was something about how Dad and Mum looked at each other that made Norma Jean think they were expecting this call, and it wasn't her Danish grandparents.

She finished washing Barry's face then said, "I'll make some more Tang." Lifting the empty two quart plastic juice pitcher from the middle of the table, she caught Gyp and Howard's eyes. "*Something's going on,*" her look told them.

Mum walked to the small entry hallway that was just off the porch, took the receiver off the brown wall-phone, and said, "Hello?" Then she stretched the long cord, opened the basement door, stepped through it and closed it behind her.

Oh shoot! Norma Jean slowly poured two packages of orange Tang into the juice pitcher, hoping she could catch a word...just ONE word of the conversation. Nothing. She brought the juice back to the table. Howard and Gyp were both watching her. With a meager little shake of her head, she sat down again between them.

Kathy placed a bowl of peaches and cream in front of each person, poured coffee for Dad and Gyp and sat down again.

"Thanks, Kathy," Dad said. Everyone else followed his lead.

Halfway through dessert, Mum sat down again. Kathy got up and poured her coffee.

Norma Jean, giving Howard his cue, kicked him under the table.

"Who was it, Mum?" he asked, looking at Norma Jean. She smiled, ever so slightly, and Howard kicked her back.

Mum said, "It was your Grandad! He says *hello* to everyone! So does Grandmum," she smiled around the table.

Norma Jean kicked Howard again. "What did he want?" Howard asked again, kicking Norma Jean, harder this time.

"Oh, he's just checking in on us. He knew that Gyp was coming and was wondering how he's enjoying the farm. I told him you were having a great summer, Gyp. Did I speak for you rightly?" Mum smiled at Gyp.

"*Très bon!*" Gyp said.

The big boys looked at him but before they could say anything, Howard said, "Very good!" then looked at the boys and continued, "Anybody knows that."

They rolled their eyes but kept silent.

Norma Jean kicked Howard again. "What else did you talk about," he almost shouted to Mum while kicking Norma Jean so hard that it got the attention of the rest of the table.

"What's going on down there?" Dad asked.

"Nothing," Norma Jean said.

"Doesn't sound like nothing to me," Dad held his coffee cup up and Kathy filled it. He spooned some cream from his bowl into his mug and added a teaspoon of sugar. "You know, Florence, we should go to B.C. and get some fruit. These peaches are delicious. I expect you'd like to can some for winter."

"I would," Mum agreed.

"Why don't you take the kids and go?" he continued. "The boys and I can hold down the fort here for a week, can't we, boys?"

"Who'll cook?" Allan asked.

"I'll ask Bedstemor to come and help out. And I'll put Bedstefar on a tractor. That north quarter of the Goldstom's place needs to be harrowed. Yup, we could use his help."

"Well, the kids can rock pick it," Les said. "I'm not."

"Yes, they can," Dad agreed, "But it can wait until the end of the summer. That land is going to stay fallow this year. What do you think, kids? Want to go to the Hiawatha?"

"YES!" Norma Jean and Howard shouted.

"Kathy?" Dad asked.

"Sure!" she said.

"I'll need a week to get everything ready," Mum said. "Let's plan for next Monday. It'll be all right if I take the station wagon?" she asked Dad.

"Do you feel confident driving through the mountains, Florence?" he asked.

"My dear," she said, "You've never asked me if I feel confident driving the grain truck, or the Versatile tractor, or the combine, or..."

Dad laughed, "I give up! I KNOW you can take that station wagon through the mountains, and have fun doing it."

"Thank you," Mum said, crossing her arms and smiling, big.

"Hey," Keith said, "I wanna go to Cranbrook!"

"With them gone, it's four less kids waiting on the dock for a ski," Dad said, winking at him.

"Cool!" Keith said. "Have fun, kids!"

Everyone cleared their own dishes, put them in the dishwasher, and the girls did the rest of the kitchen clean up.

"So, Mum," Norma Jean said, as she washed the greasy griddle, "Is there any other reason Grandad wants us to come see him?"

Mum was washing down the stove and didn't answer.

"Mum?" Norma Jean repeated.

No answer.

Kathy and Norma Jean looked at each other. "Mum?" Kathy said.

"What? I mean, pardon?" Mum said. "Did you say something?"

Norma Jean looked at her, and saw worry lines on her forehead. Kathy looked at Norma Jean and Norma Jean said, "No, Mum. It was nothing. Just complaining about this greasy mess."

Later that night, when the sun had finally set, Gyp, Howard, and Norma Jean made their beds in the backyard. Nicky joined them, on skunk patrol for the night. The boys were in the bunkhouse to their right, and the kids could hear them banging around and laughing. Kathy and Barry were in the house with Mum and Dad. The almost-full moon shone bright, and so the stars were few.

Norma Jean sat on her sleeping bag and looked at the boys. "Okay," she said, her polkdot flannel pajamas almost neon in the bright moonlight. "There's some things that need to go in our notebook." The book was on her lap, pencil in her hand. "And it's this..."

She read it aloud as she wrote:

Clue Number 16: Mum gets a mysterious phone call from Grandad, and all of a sudden we're making a visit to them. She's worried about something.

"Do you agree?" she asked Howard and Gyp after she had already written it down.

"Yup," Howard said.

"Uh-huh," Gyp agreed.

"Is there anything else?" she asked.

They all thought for a few minutes and looked at each other in silence.

"That's it," Howard finally said.

"Can't think of anything else, either," Gyp said.

Norma Jean put the notebook under her pillow and then looked over at the bunkhouse. "If that Les tries to scare us tonight and we run... DON'T let me forget to grab the notebook," she said.

"What?" Gyp sat up, "What's he gonna do?" His voice was higher-pitched than usual.

"Never mind her, Gyp," Howard said, already mostly asleep. "She's always worried about Les...he never does anything. Don't worry."

Gyp looked at Norma Jean. She shrugged.

She crawled into the sleeping bag and was grateful for the flannel lining, even if it was cows, and laid on her back to look at the moon...

The moon...THE moon...THE MOON!

She sat up and hissed to the boys, "Wake up, you guys!! I got it!!"

"What?" Howard said, crossly, "What now, Norma Jean?"

Gyp was staring at her, wide-eyed.

"The clue that's been eluding me..." she started.

"EELLUUDDIINNGG you?" Howard sounded the word out, slow and long.

"YES!" she continued, "It's the MOON! The MOON!" She could see the whites of Gyp and Howard's eyes reflected in the moonlight.

"Listen, she explained, "the great-great-grand-mère and her coondog were standing on that knoll *in the moonlight*. She WANTED us to see her. AND, I've seen Hitchcock sitting on that spruce tree outside the window at the cabin—the one right by my bed—*in the moonlight*, AND Mum said that the

MOON was an omen just like blackbirds, and broomstick straws." She pulled the notebook back out.

Clue Number 17: Great-great-grand-mère and Hitchcock are both giving us MOON omens.

Howard started laughing.

"What?" Norma Jean said, "What?"

"The creepymère and Hitchcock are MOONing us," Howard started in...laughing until he had to go pee in the trees.

Gyp joined him.

"As soon as you two are done being dorks, I have ONE more thing to add..." Norma Jean said. They came back and sat on their sleeping bags.

"Go on," Gyp said.

"Remember when Mum said she didn't know why the omens were in front of the outhouse?" she asked them.

"Yeah," they both said.

"Well, I know why," she said, looking at them.

They waited for her to continue and finally Howard said, "Enough, already, Norma Jean, WHY?"

"Because the outhouse has a crescent moon right there on the door. It's all connected."

And without another word, she laid down, turned her back to them, and went to sleep.

Chapter 10
THE VOYAGE OF THE WESTERN RED CEDAR

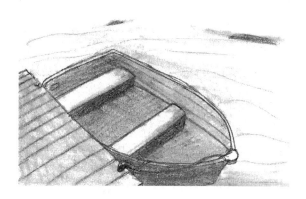

"Hurray!" Howard said as he rolled over, "Today's Saturday!"

They were back in the small cabin, having spent most of the week going back and forth between swimming in the lake and helping the boys hay.

"Every day is Saturday in the summer, silly." Norma Jean called to him from the porch steps where she and Gyp were sitting, soaking in the warm, morning sun.

"I know, but today we'll finish the haying and on Monday we go to the Hiawatha!" he yawned, "And, Mum said we could drive Old Blue to take coffee to the boys."

"She did?" Norma Jean asked, her voice rising in excitement.

N.J. Bennett

"Yup, she did. And I get to drive first." Howard joined them on the steps, shirtless as usual.

All week Norma Jean, Howard, and Gyp had been tramping the sweet alfalfa field following the hay binder, and helping to arrange the forty pound square bales on the hay wagon.

Dad's intention of asking them to *help* was more for them to see how machinery worked, what hard labour looked like, and to initiate Howard into the role that he would step into several growing years from now. Howard and Norma Jean LOVED the farm life. They taught Gyp how to look for and catch baby mice after the hay swaths had been raked, how to put on leather gloves and using teamwork and a shout of *one...two...three!* throw a hale bale onto the wagon, and how to drive the 50 horsepower Massey Ferguson tractor.

They sat on the porch steps in companionable silence. Gyp and Norma Jean were already dressed for the day and eventually Howard decided he must do the same. He wandered off to the outhouse first.

"What in the world!!" he exclaimed.

Gyp and Norma Jean looked at each other and then considering it was the OUTHOUSE, the place where mystery was seeming to take place, they ran over to see what Howard was talking about.

There, on the pine-slatted floor of the four-foot by four-foot outhouse, sat the coondog, contented as could be. He looked up at them, wagged his tail and put his head back down.

"And just how am I suppose to pee?" Howard said, hands on his hips, addressing the dog.

Gyp pointed to the trees behind the outhouse. "Those work," he said. Howard trotted off, liking the trees more than the outhouse anyway.

Norma Jean and Gyp stood in front of the open door, staring at the dog and the dog staring back at them.

Howard joined them a few minutes later and said, "Do you think Les put him in here?"

"Could be," Norma Jean said. "The tractor hasn't started yet. They're all still having breakfast. I guess the dog COULD have been here all night...but that doesn't make sense."

"Why not?" Howard asked.

"Was the door latched from the outside so that the dog couldn't get out, Howard?"

"Wait a second," Gyp interrupted. "We're missing the obvious."

Norma Jean and Howard looked at him.

"Norma Jean, did you use the outhouse this morning?" he asked.

"Uh-huh...and the dog wasn't here! Oh shoot; by the love of St Afan, I can't believe I didn't think of that first. I'm going back to drinking coffee every morning, and give me some of that chicory root," Norma Jean said.

"Which means the dog arrived here sometime in the last half-hour or so," Gyp said.

"Did YOU use the outhouse?" Norma Jean asked Gyp.

He shook his head and pointed to the trees.

"So, you're right then, sometime in the last half-hour this dog has arrived and parked himself in our outhouse," Norma Jean said.

They went to the west side of the cabin, where the window was beside Norma Jean's bed, and where they could look northwards towards Spruce Bay. Then they walked back to the outhouse and fixed their eyes on that coondog. He had rolled over...

All three of the kids gasped! There, tied around its belly was the same *gift* that Nicky had brought them.

"Hey, boy," Howard said gently as he reached down and stroked his head, "What's that ya got for us? Is this for us, eh boy?"

Gyp pulled a jackknife from one of his many pockets and handed it to Howard, who quickly cut the string and held up a narrow strip of blue silk cloth, embossed with a star, surrounded by rays. And just like Nicky's, underneath the star was a vessel in full sail with the word "Acadia" on a flag.

"This is the Acadian insignia, again!" Gyp said.

"*L'union fait la force,*" Norma Jean read, touching the red and white rosette.

And once again, Gyp pulled out the medallion from under his crew neck T-shirt. "What's going on here?" he asked.

"Oh my goodness; Oh my goodness!" Norma Jean grabbed their arms.

"What?" Howard and Gyp said at the same time.

"We've just been given permission to go through the nature-coded back door!" she exclaimed.

They gawked at her.

"Really!" she said. "Look at this dog." They did so. "He's not going ANYWHERE. In fact he's already asleep again. He LIKES it here under the crescent moon. If he really is a Catahoula Leopard coondog..."

"And he IS," Gyp interrupted.

Norma Jean nodded her head and continued, "Then he LIKES all the *gris-gris*..."

"I just knew you were gonna find a way to use that word when I heard Mum say it!" Howard laughed, "But it's okay, it's a super cool word: *gris-gris:* omens."

Norma Jean smiled. "This here dog WANTS us to go to the great-great-grand-mère's hut. He knows we won't go because we were afraid he'd howl. This insignia tied to him is permission for us to open the KEY to the nature- door. Come on! Let's go!"

"Wait!" Howard said, "I wanna drive Old Blue!"

"We'll be back before morning coffee, Howard! Come on! Get dressed!"

She ran to the cabin to pack breakfast sandwiches to eat in the Western Red Cedar. Gyp filled Nicky's bowl with water and put it at the outhouse door. They could hear Nicky barking at the big cabin as the boys started off towards the tractor and hay binder. Norma Jean yelled across the field to the boys that they would bring them morning coffee in a couple of hours. They waved acknowledgment.

And they were off...running down the trail...into the boathouse to get life jackets and oars...untying the Western Red Cedar...and pushing away from the dock. This time they rowed in a beeline straight to the reeds, SURE that they were expected. At least Norma Jean was sure. The boys were not quite so sure but were willing to take hold of an adventure if one should happen.

They pulled onto the shore, securing the rowboat to the same sturdy poplar tree, using their favorite double loop bowline knot.

"Okay," Norma Jean said, "Howard, find the key."

Howard moved back and forth and then stood still, "Right...right..." he moved his head just a little. "Right here!" He pointed and Norma Jean and Gyp came to stand in front of him.

"Okay," Norma Jean said again...

"Okay, okay! Norma Jean," Howard mocked.

"SHHH!" she said.

"I thought we didn't have to be quiet this time," Howard said.

"Well, I don't THINK we have to be quiet, but what if I'm..." she hesitated.

"WRONG?!" Howard finished, and laughed.

Meanwhile Gyp had followed the insignia and was eight trees ahead of them. "Come on, you two, for the love of St. Monica!"

"What...? Howard started.

"*Patience*." Gyp quipped, "The patron Saint for *Patience*."

Norma Jean and Howard ran up behind Gyp and followed him as he followed mark by mark through the trees.

"Oh my goodness," Norma Jean whispered.

"There you go being quiet again," said Howard, but he was whispering too.

Suddenly, they were in a ten-by-ten foot clearing. The markings had ended...and there was NO hut!

"What?" Norma Jean exclaimed. This can't be right. I'm SURE we were supposed to find the great-great-grand-mère's hut!"

They wandered clockwise around the clearing, looking at the ground and at the trees around them. Finally, Howard said, "I'm going back to the boat for breakfast," and he took off running.

"It'll truly be a work of St. Nicholas the Wonder-worker, if there's any food left," Gyp laughed. He and Norma Jean sat down in the tall grass and waited for Howard to return.

"What do you think, Gyp? Am I right-on or right-off?" Norma Jean asked him.

"I'm not sure, Norma Jean. I'm still trying to figure out if all this has any connection to my mom."

Norma Jean was silent for a moment. "Of course you are. That would be my only thought too, if I was you. Remember, Mum says you're not to worry. I'm sure it'll all make sense soon."

They both plucked a young grass shoot and started chewing it. Norma Jean lay down and looked at the tall poplar trees.

"These trees have not been topped," she said. "This is NOT the place of the hut," she sighed.

They let silence and the sound of boat motors fill their senses for the next few minutes. Mosquitoes whined and hovered over their potential lunch. Every now and then Norma Jean and Gyp would SLAP, ensuring the nasty insect never sucked blood again.

"These mosquitoes are just like vampires," Norma Jean said.

Gyp agreed, "But I don't think that's a clue."

All of a sudden Norma Jean sat up. "LOOK!" she pointed.

Howard had just come back into the clearing and was eating an apple. The boys both looked where she was pointing. There, on the east side of the clearing was a crescent moon carved into the one and only ash tree in the area

They all gathered under it, and Howard reached up and touched it. "This feels like it might have been carved pretty recently," he said. "Whaddya think it means?"

All lethargy had been thrown off and the kids vigorously searched the clearing.

"Wait a minute," Norma Jean said, "We've got to THINK!"

The boys stopped and looked at her.

"Okay..." she glanced at Howard but he kept silent. "Okay...look at the moon...it's somewhat tilted..."

Using her index finger of her right hand, she traced the outside crescent into the air. "It's almost like...almost like the bottom of the crescent is...pointing to the ground!" she exclaimed, ran over to the ash tree and looked at the ground right underneath it. Gyp and Howard joined her. They began to move the tall silvery-gold Indian prairie grass aside and search the moist terrain.

"I found it!" Gyp yelled. "Look!" They all crouched down and watched as Gyp pulled the grass and dirt away from an old and scarred cement foundation. Norma Jean and Howard helped him and after a few minutes they had unearthed what appeared to be the corner of a structure that was many, many years gone.

"Wait," Howard said, "There's more. He stood up and started kicking his rubber-soled high-top runner over the top of the cement. Slowly, words emerged as the dirt and roots cleared.

Simultaneously, they read: *L'union fait la force*. They knelt there, staring at each other.

"OKAY, Norma Jean," Howard said, "Maybe you WERE right."

"Pardon?" Norma Jean looked at Howard.

"I said, maybe..." he started to repeat.

Gyp cuffed his head and laughed and Norma Jean laughed too. Howard gave her a push and she fell back off her knees, into the soft grass. They all laughed, and realized they needed to; coondog or no, they had been scared.

Not sure what to do about this clue, they ran back to the Western Red Cedar, rowed their way back to the Nielsen beach, and ran up the trail to drive Old Blue to the boys for morning coffee and cinnamon rolls.

Norma Jean sat on the end of the tailgate and quietly pulled the notebook out of her knapsack.

The big boys were busy yapping about what girls were coming to the lake tomorrow and how they were going to get Dad to pull them behind the boat this evening so they could practice their new idea. The painted plywood disk had worked just dandy and now that they were all proficient at standing on it, they wanted to try to drop a kitchen stool off the boat, pick it up, put it on the round plywood board, and then stand on it. They hoped to have the trick ready before the girls came tomorrow afternoon.

"What are you doing there, Norma Jean?" Les said, "Writing a novel?" he laughed.

"Maybe," she said. Howard and Gyp joined her on the tailgate and watched as she wrote:

Clue Number 18: The coondog visits our outhouse, bearing the same gift that Nicky had… the Acadian insignia.

Clue Number 19: We follow the nature-lock and find the ruins of an old structure. The Acadian motto is inscribed into the cement.

Norma Jean looked at Gyp and Howard; they silently nodded. She put the notebook back in her knapsack, fastened it, and threw it in the bed of the truck.

"My turn to drive, Howard," she said as she gathered up the coffee things and put them in the truck-bed.

Howard closed the tailgate, and then he and Gyp jumped over it into the back, each taking a wheel well. Norma Jean ground the old, blue 1950 Ford truck into first, then second gear and turned its nose toward the big cabin. Every few seconds she glanced down at the hayfield that was flying by under her feet. The truck had no floorboards and it was both exciting and scary to see...

Today, Norma Jean only felt excitement.

Chapter 11
NORMA JEAN DOES SOME DEDUCING

Monday morning arrived and Dad helped pack Norma Jean, Howard, Gyp, Kathy, baby Barry, Mum, and all their luggage, into the cherry-red, 1964 Chevy II station wagon.

Gyp and Howard were sitting in the rear seat, facing out the back window of the car—games, pillows, and blankets surrounding them. They were playing *I Spy* even before Mum had driven down the laneway.

Norma Jean was in the middle seat along with several suitcases, a food basket, and her own pillow. She was reading by the time they reached the mailbox.

Baby Barry was standing between Mum and Kathy in the front seat, saying, "Bye-bye, bye-bye," over and over.

Norma Jean had hung around Mum and Dad as much as possible during the goodbyes. If Dad had last-minute instructions to give Mum about this somewhat random trip, she wanted to hear them. There were a few phrases and words that she caught, and put together with the snatches of conversation she had heard, days ago, when they had been talking beside the pickup...yes, there was definitely something going on.

She read for a few hours, then when the boys had gone to sleep in the back, and Baby Barry was asleep in his blankets on top of the suitcases beside her, and Kathy was reading, she pulled out the notebook. She'd been waiting...waiting...until the car was quiet and they were in the mountains—away from everything ordinary. She didn't have a *clue* to write down, but she did have those words, and phrases. Maybe if she saw them on paper they would make more sense. She wrote:

Things I heard Dad say: *Your mother's people; find out; don't believe; you need to go; it's nonsense;* and the most stunning of all: *TREASURE.*

Things I heard Mum say: *I'm worried; the riddle; the kids; Grandmum thinks;* and again the most stunning of all: *TREASURE.*

Now, what can I deduce from all this?

Norma Jean looked out the window at the majestic Rocky Mountains, letting the words skip around in her brain. *I need to look at all the clues again.* She ran her finger down the page as she read each one:

Clue Number 1: Our B.R.D ghost has a name and he's sleeping in the bed across the cabin: Bernard Richard Dupre. AND there's some kind of mystery associated with him.

Oh, that's right! I'd almost forgotten about that. Yes, there's something about Bernard Richard Dupre...

Clue Number 2: The coondog and the grandmother from Spruce Bay are watching us and being really, really creepy.

Yes, they definitely are, and I think they want us to KNOW it. But why hide?

Clue Number 3: OUR B.R.D. is involved in a mystery that involves a KEY.

Is there more to this KEY thing? Is there an actual KEY out there somewhere? If BOTH Mum and Dad are talking about treasure, could there be a KEY to it?

She looked around the car, feeling a little silly that she was letting her imagination get carried away. But of course, no one could hear her, so she continued to think and process the clues.

Clue Number 4: Dixie's family is from Louisiana; Grand-père knows Gyp.

How?

Clue Number 5: What is *gris-gris?*
Omens, and we're getting plenty of them.

She went through the notebook, reading all the clues in order — going over them, and over them, and over them.

OK, think, Norma Jean...that riddle...the order to my past...*if this was written in the time of Le Grand Dérangement, Père could mean...that Marie...and she must be his daughter since he signed the letter* Père...*Marie is the most recent addition to the family tree? And*...the joy to my present...*he loves her very, very much...And*... the hope for my future...*maybe she is his only child, so the generations to come will only come through her...and SHE is being shipped off to Louisiana or somewhere away from Canada...and he wants her to* remember her past...*because her past is connected with her future happiness. Well, her PAST is Acadian, and her FUTURE is away from her past...and if she doesn't remember Acadia then she won't find the treasure that was buried when they had to flee! And great-great-grand-mère is helping US to remember the past with all her gris-gris...which COULD mean there is treasure RIGHT THERE AT PINE LAKE and she wants us to find it!*

Norma Jean looked at the back of her Mum's curly brown hair.

Keep thinking, Norma Jean, keep thinking.

Barry began to stir and whimper a little.

NO! Don't wake up yet, Barry. I'm not done thinking! She reached over and smoothed his blonde hair, "It's okay, Little Manny, it's okay," she whispered.

"Oh, good," Mum said, "I've been waiting for him to wake up so I can pull over and open up that thermos of coffee."

Kathy closed her book. "And I can't believe Howard is still asleep and not eating the upholstery," Mum continued. "Hang on, Barry, I'll stop at the next picnic area."

Oh shoot. I think I'm on to something. DON'T forget!!

"What's going on?" Howard said, and he lifted his pillow-case creased face and peered over the back seat at Mum.

"We'll stop for coffee and lunch as soon as I see a pull-out, Howard. Just let Gyp sleep..." Mum said.

Too late. Howard had already pillow-pummeled him awake.

Norma Jean pulled Barry onto her lap and they looked out the window together. While everyone else was sleeping, Norma Jean and Mum had seen three moose, and a whole herd of deer. Now, she and Barry were hoping for a bear. Howard and Gyp joined them in their search.

Several miles later Mum pulled the big wagon into a shady, off-road picnic spot, designed for the weary traveler. There were several picnic tables, an outhouse, and bear-proof garbage cans.

Howard and Gyp were already lifting the back door up, before Mum had even stopped. Scrambling out, they immediately ran down to the cold mountain stream where they began splashing each other and rock hopping. Norma Jean and Barry joined them while Mum and Kathy spread the red and white checked table cloth and laid out the lunch things.

There were cold roast beef sandwiches on homemade rye bread, sandwich spread on all but one. Norma Jean didn't like sandwich spread. Chocolate cake, the thick dark icing sticking to the wax paper, apples, raspberries, raw carrots, and a jar of juice. Coffee for Mum and Gyp. Everyone ate at their leisure, Mum not worrying about a "family" lunch.

Norma Jean watched Mum take Barry down to the stream to wash his messy face and hands. She followed.

"So, Mum," she called after her, "has anyone ever looked for treasure at the lake?"

"Oh, goodness, no," she said. "What makes you ask?"

Howard and Gyp had been wading in the stream close by, and Howard piped up, "Yeah, why, Norma Jean? Did you think of something?"

"Not sure yet," she said mysteriously. "Might have. I need to think some more. I'll tell you tonight."

"I guess if we're going to be at the Hiawatha by tonight we'd better let this magical picnic come to an end," Mum said.

Normally, there would have been grumbling, but everyone was anxious to move on and see Grandad and Grandmum. They packed up the picnic, changed places in the car, and got back on the winding mountain highway.

Norma Jean commenced thinking...

Okay, what IF there was family treasure that got passed down from generation to generation, but somewhere along the line someone dropped the ball and forgot to pass it along...could our B.R.D. have left treasure behind at the cabin when he disappeared? And does the great-great-grand-mère think that too? Is she WILLING us, through all her gris-gris, to search for the treasure? And here Norma Jean stopped and sighed out loud.

"What's the matter, Norma Jean?" Howard asked.

"Nothing," she said rather shortly. Feeling bad, she added, "I'll tell you later."

I've got to go back to the clues. She opened the notebook.

<u>Clue Number 6:</u> The great-great-grand-mère's hut is camouflaged by a nature-coded backdoor and we found the KEY.

We found the nature-coded backdoor, just like great-great-grand-mere wanted us to...we know that Gyp's family and our family both have a historical letter (riddle) that was stuffed into a French bible...

She chewed her pencil.

And now I'm stuck. Why do we both have this? Think, Norma Jean, think...

She was sitting in the far-back rear seat, watching the road behind them, happy that no one was watching her.

What if...what if...no, not what if...start again. Gyp's family is connected to ours from way back to the time of the Le Grand Dérangement...now, what if...what if his mum and dad are finding our family treasure right now at St. Croix...then there wouldn't be any at the lake...but WHY is great-great-grand-mère giving us these clues?

Before she could stop herself, she turned around and blurted out, "Hey, Gyp! Do you think your mum and dad have found the key to OUR family's treasure?"

"Maybe mine, but not yours," Gyp said, surprised at the sudden question.

"What do you mean?" Norma Jean responded, even more surprised at Gyp's answer than he had been by her question.

Gyp continued by asking, "Have you ever gone to an Acadian Day Festival?"

"A what?" she asked.

"August 15th, Acadian Day," Gyp explained.

"Mum?" Norma Jean asked.

"No, we haven't. I've thought about it. There's a big Acadian population in Edmonton and I've always wanted to go up for the celebration but it's too close to harvest. We're just too busy," Mum said.

"Well, in Louisiana, it's a really, really big deal. Every August 15th on National Acadia Day, all the Acadian families carry the insignia through the streets of Lafayette, to the town square where there's a huge party with all kinds of food and..."

"What kind of food?" Howard asked.

"Not now, Howard," Norma Jean said.

Gyp looked at Howard and started to sing, "Jambalaya, crawfish pie, filé gumbo..." then said, "don't tell your dad I know that song."

Norma Jean and Howard looked at him blankly and Mum and Kathy laughed.

"So anyway...?" Norma Jean asked, looking at Gyp.

"They have games for the kids and we all search for our family's treasure. Every family has its own treasure and if the treasure never got passed down through the generations, then that family lost its treasure."

"Okay, thanks," Norma Jean turned around and looked out the back window again.

"Weirdo," Howard whispered to Gyp, but Gyp didn't laugh this time.

"Howard..." Mum warned from the front seat.

"I know. Sorry," he said.

"I'm just gonna think for a bit more, then I'll play Battleship with you," Norma Jean said.

"Great!" Howard said, "We'll get it ready. Wanna play, Kathy?"

"Sure!" she responded.

Norma Jean went back to her notebook.

I'm gonna skip ahead to...

Clue Number 19: We follow the nature-lock and find the ruins of an old structure. The Acadian motto is inscribed into the cement.

So, why is there a foundation by the great-great-grand-mère's hut with the Acadian motto: "Strength through Unity"? Maybe...maybe if a family no longer passed on the treasure they...they...they what?

"OH!" she hadn't meant to say that out loud.

"What?" Howard asked.

"Never mind," Gyp said. "Keep showing me how to make this Battleship game."

OH I KNOW!! If the oldest child in the family doesn't pass on the key to the treasure then the family is no longer united. And the great-great-grand-mère cares about this because she is Acadian and wants her people, ALL Acadians, to stay united.

Norma Jean looked over her shoulder, hoping no one was watching her. Gyp was. He smiled at her. She turned back around.

Oh, this is just...stupid...STILL...it kinda makes sense. Keep thinking, Norma Jean, keep thinking...

She picked up the notebook and wrote:
Questions I need to ask Grandmum:

1. Is our family treasure lost and if so was it B.R.D.'s generation that lost it?

2. Do you think the KEY is actually a KEY to a treasure or is it merely symbolic?

3. If there is a missing KEY to our family treasure do you have any idea where it is?

And now, I will play Battleship...

"B", "4"...

The battle began.

Chapter 12
HIAWATHA BOUND

They arrived at the Hiawatha Motel late that night. All the kids were asleep and Grandad and Grandmum helped a very tired family get settled into one of the motel cabins.

"We'll talk in the morning, Florence," Grandmum said, "Sleep in, if you can."

Norma Jean heard Mum laugh softly, "Somehow, I don't think that's going to happen. Goodnight, *Mère*."

Mère? Norma Jean had never heard her mum call HER mum, *Mère*. But there it was, clear as that mountain stream they drank from this afternoon. Her Grandmum was Mère.

"Mum?" Norma Jean said.

"Not now, Norma Jean," Mum answered.

Norma Jean could hear the weariness in her voice. She HAD just driven five kids across the mountains for the past ten hours. *I'd better let her sleep...* She did the same.

The mountain air was fresh and cold in the motel cabin when Norma Jean awoke the next morning. She snuggled deeper under the feather duvet, pulling a little from Kathy who was asleep beside her. Mum and Barry were already up and gone; Norma Jean was surprised she'd not heard them leave. *I must have been tired.* She pulled the covers a little more to her side and sensing no resistance, she realized that Kathy was up and gone, also.

She used the washroom, then sat up in bed and read until Gyp and Howard woke up.

"'Bout time!" she said. "The others have already gone up to the coffee shop. Grandmum is sure to be making something delicious." As soon as she said that she wished she'd hadn't. Before Howard could get out the door, she stopped him. "Wait," she called. "I wanna tell you about what I was thinking yesterday."

Howard came and sat on the end of her bed, "Okay, but hurry up. I'm starved."

Norma Jean showed them the notebook with the words and phrases she'd overheard from Dad and Mum and then told how she deduced—except she didn't use that word because she just didn't want to deal with any teasing this morning—that this *mystery* might have to do with their family line losing their treasure.

"What do you think?" she asked them, somewhat nervous about their responses.

"I don't think it's stupid, Norma Jean," Howard said.

"Neither do I," Gyp agreed. "You two should go talk to your grandparents."

They were silent. They didn't know these grandparents well, not like Bedstefar and Bedstemor who had always been around them. Grandad was a wee bit...well... he scared them just a little.

"You're right," Norma Jean said. "We should. And we will."

"Now, can we eat?" Howard said.

They left the cabin and ran across the gravel driveway to the gas station and coffee shop.

The motel had been built by Grandad in 1949 and Norma Jean and Howard were somewhat in awe of it. Growing up on the farm, they filled the car, truck, and machinery gas tanks from a large steel drum that was raised up on a pedestal in the backyard. The *town* gas station was a thing of mystery. As was the coffee shop. Rarely had they ever been in such a place, let alone been allowed behind the lunch counter to serve pie and coffee. It was almost like the Kressge's counter that Mum sometimes took them to on library day. There was a long narrow counter with a dozen red vinyl swing stools spaced evenly in front of it. Behind the counter was where Grandmum conjured her spells: she made her milkshakes—chocolate, strawberry, vanilla, or banana; stored her pies—lemon meringue, saskatoon, blackberry, rhubarb, and chocolate cream; crafted her sandwiches —ham, turkey, beef, egg salad, tuna salad; and handled her grill—hamburgers, cheeseburgers, steaks, veal cutlets, pork chops.

The kids walked in the back door, through Grandmum's working kitchen, past the motel laundry room, and into the café. They could see Grandad out the front window, filling a bread truck with gas. On the counter, there was what appeared to be a fresh delivery of bread.

Norma Jean walked behind the counter and gave her grandmum a hug, as did Howard.

"What's this you got here, Pearl?" gruffed a burly man hulked over the counter, devouring french toast and too much maple syrup.

"Florence is here for a visit," Grandmum said. "And these are two of her seven scallewags...and this is...?" She looked at Gyp.

"I'm Bernard Richard Dupre," Gyp said.
"But please call me Gypsy."

Norma Jean was watching Grandmum and she was *positive* Grandmum looked out the window at Grandad, and they locked eyes for a split second.

"Well, that's quite the handle, little fella," the chap at the end of the counter laughed. "How 'bout some more coffee, Pearl?"

Norma Jean looked at Grandmum and she smiled, "Thank you, Norma Jean. Don't be too much help or I'll keep you."

Norma Jean carefully picked up the glass-bottom coffee pot and poured the portly trucker more coffee.

"Just keep her, Pearl," he said. "Florence'll never miss just one!" Norma Jean smiled because she knew she had to be polite to the Hiawatha customers, but she hoped he would leave soon.

There were three empty stools at the farthest end of the counter from the trucker and Grandmum motioned for the kids to sit down. "French toast is on the menu for breakfast this morning." She looked at Gyp, "*ça va*?"

"*Fort à propos*, Grand-mère!" Gyp responded.

Norma Jean and Howard gaped at him.

Grandmum poured Gyp coffee, without asking, and Norma Jean could smell the chicory root in it. Then she poured orange juice for Norma Jean and Howard.

"Where's the others?" Howard asked.

"I've been swamped and I asked your mum and Kathy if they would go clean cabin 12. My girl, Hazel, can't come in this morning. It won't take the two of them very long. And your Auntie Donna and Auntie Marie have grabbed Baby Barry and they are long gone. I think they're in the garden."

Norma Jean and Howard smiled at each other. They had two unmarried aunties that still lived here and they were a TON of fun.

Grandmum started cracking eggs, mixed milk and cinnamon into them, and then she took the day-old bread that was in the tin bread-keeper, dipped both sides in the batter, and was just about to place it in the sizzling butter when Norma Jean saw her glance up and look outside at Grandad again. Ever so slightly, Grandad nodded.

"I'm going to change the menu," Grandmum said abruptly. I've got a new pancake batter recipe, and guess what...you're my guinea pigs."

"Great!" Howard smiled. "I might need four pancakes to taste and then four more to be sure. Stack them up, Grandmum."

Grandmum bent down to a small cooler and pulled out a yellow glass bowl that was filled with freshly-made pancake batter. She took a wooden spoon, stirred it up, adjusted the temperature of the grill and dropped another dollop of butter on it. Then she turned her back to the kids and spread the pancake batter on the sizzling grill. She pulled thick white plates from the shelf above her and laid one in front of each kid. Watching for the air bubbles in the batter to tell her it was time to turn them, she flipped the pancakes. One minute later, she laid a pancake onto each child's plate.

At first, Norma Jean was embarrassed for Grandmum. She usually made perfect everything! These pancakes were very, very oddly shaped.

Thankfully, Howard didn't hesitate to ask, "Cool, Grandmum! What shapes are these supposed to be? Sorry, I can't tell."

"Well," Grandmum glanced outside again. Grandad was staring at them. She pointed to Norma Jean's plate, "This one is a crescent moon." She pointed to Gyp's plate, "This one is a blackbird." She pointed to Howard's plate, "And this one is a cow." She looked at them. They looked at her.

"Grandmum!" Norma Jean whispered. "You know about the *gris-gris!*"

"So it's true!" Grandmum whispered, and looked through the window at Grandad.

"What's true?" Norma Jean asked.

"We've been wrong all these years..." Grandmum started. She walked out the front door and she and Grandad stood in the shade of the big billboard that read *Hiawatha Motel, Gas & Café*, and talked.

Finally, Howard said, "Do you think she'll make me another pancake?"

"Patience..." Gyp started.

Howard interrupted, "Ya mean like Saint Monica? The patience of Saint Monica?"

"What?" Gyp looked at him surprised.

"You told me that one already."

Gyp laughed, and shoved Howard off his stool. "You're a gas, Howard. You really are."

"Shhh you guys," Norma Jean said to them, not giving a flip about any virtues Saint Monica might bestow upon her. "What is going on here?" She walked to the front of the café and opened the door, just a crack. Maybe, just maybe she'd be able to hear...

Grandmum saw her. "Will you watch the counter for me, Norma Jean? I need to go to the back kitchen and have a look at that soup I've got going. If you need help, just holler."

"Okay, Grandmum!" Norma Jean answered.

Grandmum disappeared around the corner of the café. Norma Jean went back in and started wiping the counter down, not sure if she wished someone would come in or not. Being here reminded her of when she and Howard used to play store in the basement, except this was real. But what was MORE real was that something about *gris-gris* had weirded Grandmum and Grandad out.

And still they hadn't said "hello" to Grandad. And still Grandad worked outside, lifting the hoods and checking the oil of the few cars and trucks that passed their way and pulled into the Hiawatha Motel and Gas Station.

"Do you think we should go out there and say 'hello'?" Howard whispered to Norma Jean.

"Sheesh. I don't know. Let's wait for Mum," she said, glancing out the window at Grandad. "What in the world is going on here? And why are we all whispering?"

Right before the giggles had a chance to root, Norma Jean and Howard heard the door ting as it opened. Looking up they saw that it was Gyp, who had gone outside and was walking over to Grandad.

"What's *BERNARD* doing?" Howard asked.

"I wish I knew," Norma Jean replied.

They watched as Gyp went up to Grandad, and put his hand out. Grandad looked up from the hood he was under and then closed the lid. He banged on it, waved, and stepped aside so the driver could leave. He said something to Gyp, wiped his hands on the towel he was carrying and they shook hands. They could see Gyp say something to which Grandad nodded and pointed to the back of the motel, east, towards the mountain that reared up tall and cold behind the cabins.

Gyp walked away.

"Why doesn't he wait for us?" Howard asked, running to the front window to look out. "He's going behind the garage!"

Grandmum came out from the back kitchen. "Go!" she said, "Go! Follow him! Out the back door, right now!"

The kids scampered through the empty coffee shop, through the laundry room, where Kathy and Mum were, through the back kitchen, and slammed the screen door. They could see Gyp disappear behind the cabins, heading toward the creek that moated the mountain. They ran.

"Gyp!" Howard called, "Wait for us!" They ran faster.

Norma Jean was only one Mother-May-I step behind him, and they overtook him just as he was about to cross the creek and head up a narrow ravine and into the unyielding mountain. Gyp turned, sat on a large flat rock, and waited for them to join him there.

"What are you doing?" Norma Jean panted. "Why didn't you wait for us? What did Grandad tell you?" Her questions tumbled out.

Gyp turned to look at them. "I figured it out. I know why they said they've been wrong all these years."

"And would you care to divulge your new-found knowledge with us..." Norma Jean asked, an edge to her voice. "...and why you went sprinting off without us?"

Howard looked at her and her eyes demanded his silence. Not the time for teasing. Not the time.

"Your Grandad is on his way here. He'll tell you," Gyp said.

"I highly doubt it," Howard said, frankly. "He hasn't even said 'hello' to us yet."

"He will," Gyp said confidently. He got up, looked around him and started up the ravine. Howard and Norma Jean followed him. He came to a small ten-by-ten foot clearing, surrounded by tall spruce trees and one ash tree. They gazed around the clearing, then looked at one another, wide-eyed.

"Hey!" Howard said, voicing their thoughts, "I recognize this!" He immediately walked over to the ash tree and looked up. There was the crescent moon pointing downwards. As if in a flashback of a dream, they got down on their hands and knees and dug. Sure enough, they unearthed a cement corner of a foundation, and inscribed on it was...

"*L'union fait la force*," Norma Jean said aloud. "Strength through Unity."

Howard sat down, "I really wish I knew what was goin' on here," he said.

"Yeah, me too," Norma Jean joined Howard.

Just then Grandad pushed through into the clearing and perched himself on a rock that was placed just opposite the crescent moon. Without a word he pulled a pipe and a pouch of tobacco out of his denim shirt pocket, he packed it, tamped it, and lit it. The children stared at Grandad but he didn't acknowledge their presence. Out of his coverall bib pocket he pulled a wooden ashtray, with Hiawatha painted in red on the side. He held the pipe in his right hand, and the ashtray in his left hand. Then, still without looking at the children, he started talking:

"Your grandmum and I didn't know that Gypsy was the age-old nickname for Bernard Richard Dupre until your mum told us on the phone a week or so ago." He pulled and sucked on his pipe. "All these years I've been entertaining bands of traveling gypsies, here in this clearing, waiting for someone to know the *gris-gris* signs. And then today," he paused and his steely cold black eyes stared at them, "someone knew the signs, all of them."

Norma Jean and Howard glanced at each other, too scared to talk.

Grandad ran his gnarled hand through his greying, wavy hair and continued, "You see, your Grandmum's family lost their Cajun treasure. We don't know exactly what generation forgot the *hope for the future*..."

Howard and Norma Jean glanced at each other again. *Grandad knows the riddle.*

"...but somewhere along the way, the key has been lost. This land," he gestured, with his pipe, to the clearing, "has been part of your grandmum's people for as long as she can remember. As has the property at Pine Lake, which used to include the land on which Spruce Bay is now. The LaBlanc family acquired that land from Bernard Richard Dupre, just before his family died, and he disappeared. There is an Acadian monument," Grandad nodded toward the foundation stone, "on that property too."

The children all nodded but stayed silent.

"All Acadian families remember their past with this foundation stone," Grandad continued. His voice became quiet, "But your Grandmum's family have lost the key...they have lost the key...I thought I could find it for her, but I haven't been able to find the right Gypsy." Here Grandad stared at Gyp who stared steadfastly back at him.

Still, no one asked him any questions. He moved his gaze away from Gyp and continued, "Your

Grandmum has a note that was included with her. Stuffed into..."

Here, Norma Jean couldn't help herself and gave Howard a little elbow push. Grandad had ALSO used the word *stuffed*.

"Stuffed into the French Bible was the riddle from Père, and a note that read..." here Grandad paused, and looked at Gyp again, "Gypsy has the key and will know the *gris-gris*." He looked away again, "And that was all. And all these years I've been looking for a Gypsy who knows the *gris-gris*. Today, I found him."

Grandad tapped his pipe into the ashtray, stood up, and without another word or glance, left the clearing.

Chapter 13
BOOKS ARE MY FRIENDS

"Hit it!" Keith yelled to Dad, who was driving the boat, and the 60-horse-power motor whined as Keith dropped off the dock and landed on one ski. He hung on to the ski rope, letting the boat drag him through the water, until the labouring motor boat pulled him upright. Back and forth across the boat-wake he flew. Gyp, Norma Jean, and Howard were in the boat, spotting the skier in case he fell. The wind pummeled and teased everything around them. It was too loud to talk, but not too loud to smile, and smile they did—all of them, even Dad and Keith.

The younger kids had been skiing and tubing all day and now it was the boys' turn. Dad had taken the day off while the boys finished some errands at

166

the farm, and he had given the kids his full attention. When the trio weren't in the boat they had flippers on, and were swimming back and forth in front of Bedstfar and Bedstemor, who were watching from lawn chairs. The grandparents didn't know about the flippers and Norma Jean and Howard loved to hear the exclamations, in Danish, of what amazing swimmers they were. They knew it was deceitful, but really, did it matter?

They were glad to be back at the lake. Even though they loved the gas station, summer was so short and lake days were cherished. Grandmum and Grandad had promised to come to Alberta and join the family for Acadian Day. No more answers and a whole lot more questions were the only thing Norma Jean, Howard, and Gyp had brought back with them.

That evening the three of them were sitting on the end of the pier, feet dangling in the warm water, watching the residue of the 10PM summer sunset. The rest of the family had already gone up to bed, and they were enjoying the quiet hum of crickets and the feeling of being alone in a great big world. They were not enjoying the constant hum of mosquitoes, but mosquitoes were a given and the kids were well-sprayed with repellent.

"Okay," Norma Jean said, gently kicking her feet and watching the ripples disappear into infinity. "Let's go over what we've got." She reached behind her and pulled the notebook out of her knapsack. The sun was fast waning, but the moon was waxing and she could still read the page.

"We have another clue," she said. "And only one. I can't believe that we only came home with one clue. Oh well, here it is:

<u>Clue Number 20:</u> Grandad confirmed that B.R.D. and Gypsy somehow hold the KEY to the lost family treasure."

"Is it OUR Gypsy or is it just ANY Gypsy?" Norma Jean said, looking at Gyp.

"Only a B.R.D Gypsy. We learned that from Grandad," Howard said.

"I don't get it," Gyp said. "I don't know anything about your family's lost treasure. Really, I don't." He sighed. "It's not THIS Gypsy."

Norma Jean glanced over at him. His skin had become golden, and he had, weeks ago, succumbed to the Saturday night crew cut. She could barely remember feeling a little bit uncomfortable around him. Then she saw it. The letter poking out from his back cargo-shorts pocket.

"Hey, Gyp," she said, "Did you get a letter from your folks?"

Gyp slapped his back pocket, "Oh crap. How'd I forget that?" He pulled the letter out and held it up to the moonlight. "Yes, I did!"

Norma Jean thought back to the beginning of the summer when Gyp's black eyes had beaded with tears at the sight of a letter from his folks. And now, he'd gone the whole day forgetting about it. *I'm so glad he's been happy here.*

Gyp tore the envelope open, and again, tilted it toward the moon. Norma Jean could see a page covered in well-styled hand writing. He read it silently for a few moments then whistled softly. "Far out!" he said.

"What? What's far out?" Howard asked.

"This!" Gyp held up the letter and turned his face toward Norma Jean and Howard. "Listen!"

He turned the page toward the moonlight and read:

Dearest Gypsy,

My goodness, how the summer has flown and how we've missed you!

"I'm just gonna skip this first part," Gypsy said, and Norma Jean could feel, not see his face reddening. "It's just my mom..."

He continued a moment later:

Things are moving ahead here and it looks like we will, indeed, open the Bernard Richard Dupre Museum here in St. Croix. There have been many interesting artifacts found at a dig just outside the area where the museum is to be located. The most interesting is that we have found a treasure box to which the key we found at the beginning of the summer, fits! It almost seems too good to be true. It most certainly belongs to one of the families who had to bury their treasure and flee during Le Grand Dérangement. It will be archived and placed in the museum.

"What?" Howard exclaimed, "Lucky them."

"Do you think it could be our lost family treasure?" Norma Jean asked weakly.

"Not likely," Gyp said. Then he turned to look at her. "Sorry, Norma Jean. Really I am."

They sat there in silence for several more minutes, then the exertions of the day started to play havoc with their eyelids and they found themselves yawning and sighing.

"We'd better go up to bed before we end up just laying back on the dock and calling it good!" Norma Jean said. She got up and tugged at the boys' shoulders. "Come on, guys. Let's hit the sack."

She led the way up the shadowed trail past the darkened big cabin, and down the dirt lane toward the small cabin.

They walked up the porch steps, and Gyp held open the screen door for Norma Jean and Howard. Before he went in, he stood on the porch and looked at the moon, one last time. He sighed. "I'm gonna miss this place."

The coondog howled and Gyp shivered. "I'm not gonna miss that creepy midnight howl. That's for sure." He came into the cabin, letting the screen door slam behind him.

They snuggled under quilts, said goodnight to each other, and silence filled the crevices of the creaky cabin.

Norma Jean lay in her bed, thinking, and feeling a little bit down. It really had seemed that a lost family treasure was going to be part of her summer, and now it all seemed ridiculous.

She looked out the window and watched as the summer breeze waved and bowed through the pine trees. She tossed and turned, waiting for the sleepiness that had engulfed her at the pier to come back. It didn't. She sighed some more, rolled over, then over again, and over again. Swiveling her body to find a more comfortable position she finally settled on her right side.

The cabin was awash in moonlight and Norma Jean studied the small room. It was all so familiar to her. The initials in the window frame, the cast iron stove with the flue that went through the roof, the wooden table on which she delighted to change table cloths, the shelf with plates, mugs, cutlery, the tea kettle, the coffee pot, the other two beds with snoring boys, the bookshelf...

Her eyes rested on the bookshelf—the bookshelf that she had been giving whispered summer promises to for years. *I'll come to you one day. I will. I promise. Don't leave or feel left out. It's just that there are so many other things to do at the lake.* She kept staring at the books, going through each one spine by spine, making individual promises. The moonlight cooperated by singling the shelf out and directing Norma Jean's attention to it. She could hear the boys' heavy breathing so she knew they were sleeping.

"*Moby Dick*," she whispered quietly. "*Aesop's Fables, The Hound of the Baskervilles, The Jungle, A Little Princess, The Scarlet Pimpernel, Kim, Peter Pan, The Wind in the Willows*, a French Bible..." she stopped.

"The French Bible..." she looked around the cabin. Yes, the boys were definitely sleeping. She slipped out of bed, crept across the pinewood floor and stood, looking up at the shelf. She ran her finger along the book-spines, just like she had done a thousand times before. Her finger stopped at the French Bible .

She looked around the cabin again. *I have never, ever pulled you from the shelf. I'm sorry. I should've opened you years ago. But tonight I'm going to fix that. You and I are going to become friends. Right now.* She reached up and slowly pulled the book off the shelf. The dust made her immediately sneeze and she glanced over her shoulder to the boys. No movement. Not even a twitch.

Norma Jean blew the dust from the top of the book and took it back to her bed. She sat, leaning against the window frame, letting the moonlight work its magic and open the secrets of script.

The book was old, very old. In fact, 1753 read the copyright notice on the first page. The damp heaviness and musty odor of the ancient tome put Norma Jean's very soul in awe.

History, this is history, and I am holding it.

She slowly turned another page. There, folded and placed in what Norma Jean assumed to be Genesis, even though her French was lousy, was a piece of paper.

Norma Jean took a fleeting look out the window, half expecting to see the great-great-grand-mère peering over her shoulder. Of course, there was nothing, and no one, there.

She laid the Bible on her bed and held the paper up to the moonlight. It was old; she didn't think it was as old as the Bible, but it was old. *WHY haven't I looked at this Bible before?!*

Carefully she opened the folded sheet. There, in the most beautiful handwriting she had ever seen was the age-old riddle:

My dear Marie,
You are the order to my past;
You are the joy of my present;
You are the hope for my future.
The key to future happiness
is remembering your past.
If you do not, the key is not for you,
but for another.
Love, Père

She whispered the riddle aloud.

Why are YOU here in THIS French Bible? Did you belong to B.R.D.?

Norma Jean reached behind her and traced her finger absently over the B.R.D. on the window frame. *What did you do with the family treasure, B.R.D.? Did you bury it before you disappeared? And why on earth did you leave a message with Grandmum's family about Gypsy?*

Norma Jean looked up, thinking, and then quickly folded the letter back the way it was when she found it in the Bible. Looking at it again she saw that there, on the front of the letter was inscribed the name, "Gypsy." It was barely visible, having lost its inky luster from years of being *stuffed* into this French Bible.

"This letter most definitely belonged to our B.R.D.," Norma Jean said out loud.

"What?" Howard said.

"Sheesh, Howard!" Norma Jean said. "You just scared the livin' daylights out of me. How long have you been awake?"

"Ever since you bumped my bed a few minutes ago. What are you doing?" he said, propping himself up on his elbows.

"I can't sleep," she said. "And that bookshelf started calling my name..."

"How can a bookshelf call your..." Howard started.

"Never mind, Howard, and be quiet. You'll wake up Gyp," she said.

"Yeah, ya don't wanna do that!" Gyp yawned and rolled over to look at them. "Is it morning already?"

"Well the moonlight might be a big hint, but no, it's not morning," Norma Jean said, "I just couldn't sleep."

"So she thought she heard the bookshelf call her name..." Howard started.

"Howard! Never mind," Norma Jean said. She carefully picked up the Bible in her right hand, and the letter in her left hand. "Look, you guys," she said, holding them up. "I found the family riddle in this 1753 French Bible. It's been right here on our bookshelf all this time, and I haven't made friends with it yet. I feel terrible."

"Norma Jean, books don't care..." Howard said.

"Yes, Howard. They do. Books are my friends and they care. Tonight I made friends with this French Bible and it shared its secret with me."

"Oh brother," Howard sighed.

Gypsy got out of bed, his flannel pajamas not looking as new as they did at the beginning of the summer. He walked across the cabin and sat on the end of Norma Jean's bed.

"Can I see it?" he asked.

Without a word, she handed him her treasures. Gyp gently took the book and the unfolded paper. He laid the Bible down on Norma Jean's comforter and opened the letter.

My dear Marie,
You are the order to my past;
You are the joy of my present;
You are the hope for my future.
The key to future happiness
is remembering your past.
If you do not, the key is not for you,
but for another.
Love, Père

"Not again!" Howard said, sitting fully up in bed now.

"Yes, and I think THIS letter belongs to our B.R.D.," Norma Jean pointed to the etching in the window frame.

"It certainly could be," Gyp said.

"Especially because if you look at the front of that folded page it's got the name, *Gypsy,* written on it." Norma Jean pointed to it.

"It sure does," Gyp said, looking where Norma Jean indicated.

You are the order to my past;

"Let me see it," Howard reached across to Norma Jean's bed. Gyp handed the letter to Norma Jean and she handed it to Howard.

"Be careful with it, Howard," she said.

"Whaddya think I'm gonna do, Norma Jean? Eat it?" Howard mumbled. He opened it up and read it, one more time. When he was finished, they all stared at each other, the moonlight favouring them with sight. Howard handed it back to Norma Jean and she opened it one more time.

"So, our B.R.D. lost the family treasure; at least we think he did, and great-great-grand-mère is sending us *gris-gris,* for some reason that we have yet to figure out, and we know the key to the treasure is somehow connected with the name, Gypsy..." she looked at the letter again, holding it up to the window so the moonlight shone on the seasoned, yellowed paper.

"Hey!" she said, "Look at this," she pointed to the word, 'past.' the 's' has been underlined!"

Gyp and Howard both said, "Let me see."

"I will, but just a minute," Norma Jean said. She tilted the paper so the light was full on it. "And here," she pointed again. "The letter 'o' in the word 'joy' is underlined!"

Howard got out of his bed and came and sat beside Gyp. "S, O," Howard said.

"Keep looking!" Gyp said, leaning forward. "The 't' in 'future...the 'e' in 'key'...and the 'v' in 'love'!"

"S, O, T, E, V," Howard said, slowly. "That doesn't mean anything."

Suddenly Gyp stood up and slapped his forehead. "Yes, it does!" he almost yelled. "It DOES!" He ran over and stood in front of the cast iron stove. "It spells STOVE! Move the letters around and it spells STOVE!"

Norma Jean carefully picked up the Bible and the letter and jumped off her bed to join Gyp. She laid the treasures on the table and stood with Gyp in front of the stove. Howard hop-scotched from Norma Jean's bed, onto his bed, and then onto the floor in front of the stove. They stared at it in silence. It was silent too.

After a few moments, Howard said, "I'm getting hungry. Is it breakfast time yet?"

Norma Jean got the notebook out and quickly scribbled:

Clue Number 21:

My dear Marie,
You are the order to my past;
You are the joy of my present;
You are the hope for my future.
The key to future happiness
is remembering your past.
If you do not, the key is not for you,

but for another.
Love, Père

We solved the letter's riddle: S.T.O.V.E.

Chapter 14
A CLUE HIDDEN IN PLAIN VIEW

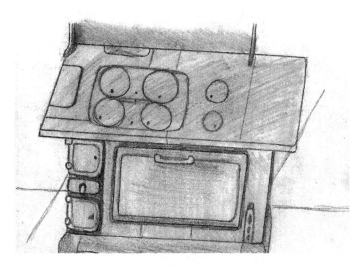

The kids were feeling the pressure of the summer coming to a close, and they still hadn't discovered the secret of the stove, if indeed there even was one. They had gone over every square inch, looking for some kind of clue to a key—but there was nothing. It was just a plain old cast iron stove.

By now the clearing by the great-great-grand-mère's hut had become a regular Western Red Cedar outing, picnic and flippers included. They had never seen the old woman up close but sometimes they found a few oranges waiting for them there, or a small paper bag of chicory; little things that made them know they were welcome. But where or what the key to the treasure was...they had no idea.

Grandad and Grandmum came as promised for Acadian Day and they all travelled to Edmonton. They wandered around the replica Acadian Village, marveling at the homes constructed with wooden pegs, mud walls, hand-hewn cypress timbers—brought from Louisiana—and the high-peaked roofs.

Weavers demonstrated their craft using white Louisiana cotton blended with brown cotton from Mexico. Blankets and clothes hung on wooden racks, begging admiration.

A blacksmith shop built with weathered cypress boards—again shipped from Louisiana—boasted its wares with anvil, forge, and bellows pounding, hissing, and blowing. Tools, nails, horseshoes, and hinges were scattered around the shop, confirming the importance of the blacksmith's job. Tongs, pinchers, hammers...all ringing a true Cajun tune.

At one point Gyp surprised them all by jumping into a dance circle and immediately finding a partner. They danced *Le Papillon* (The Butterfly), *La Danse Miroire* (The Mirror Dance), The Cajun Jitterbug, and The Cajun two-step—button box accordion and fiddle dominating the happy Zydeco sound that had been created and preserved by the Acadian people. It was a regular *Cajun Fais Do-Do*, and Norma Jean and Howard drank it all in like Louisiana sweet tea.

They ate; oh, they ate! Handmade smoked boudin sausage; filé gumbo, filled with okra and thickened with dried sassafras leaves; jambalaya with rice, chicken, shrimp, and hot peppers; rice and gravy stirred into a cast iron pot and simmered over an open fire; crawfish boil that had been dumped onto a large newspaper-covered table and sucked by hungry participants; fried catfish lightly breaded in cornmeal; and Creole cream cheese ice-cream made in a wooden bucket using ice and salt. The senses overloaded with pleasure and the whole family willingly became *Howard* for the day, and ate to their heart's content.

"Hey, Mum," Norma Jean said, "can we wander off by ourselves for a while?"

Mum looked at Dad; he looked around the Exhibition grounds and said, "I think that'll be all right, kids. Just watch out for nitwits, and stay together."

"Thanks!" Norma Jean, Howard, and Gyp said together. And as if reading each other's minds they turned back to the blacksmith shop.

"Are you thinking what I'm thinking?" Norma Jean asked the boys.

"I sure hope not," Howard mocked, "But maybe just this once, I am."

"The blacksmith can help us figure out the mystery of that blame stove!" Gyp said, "Is that what you're thinking?"

Both Norma Jean and Howard looked at him and nodded. "Let's go!" Gyp continued, and off they went, running.

They stood on the fringes of the makeshift shop, watching and listening. The crowd was too big for them to feel comfortable taking the attention of the blacksmith. After several minutes, the heavily syncopated Zydeco music caught the ears of the crowd and they moved on.

The bearded blacksmith watched them go and then stood, stretched his back, took his thick brown leather apron off, hung it on a wooden nail and smiled at the kids. "*Bonjour!*" he said.

"*Bonjour!*" they all said back.

"You seem interested in what I'm doing here. That's a nice treat for me. Usually the kids like the music and food better than a grimy old blacksmith shop. Not that I blame them," he laughed. "The smell of that crawfish pie makes my mouth water nonstop! All I get to do is make the cast iron pots they cook all that stuff in."

The kids looked at him and smiled. He didn't seem like one of the *nitwits* Dad told them to watch out for.

"Can we ask you some questions?" Norma Jean ventured.

"Can you ask me some questions! Well, that would be far out!" He sat down and gulped hungrily from a pottery water flask. "*Bon!*" he said, wiping his mouth, "Now, how can I help you?"

The kids looked at each other but before one of them spoke, Gyp nodded his head, almost imperceptibly, toward the right. Norma Jean and Howard followed his directive. There was Grandad— standing about ten feet away, watching them. He had exchanged his overalls for dark denim pants and a navy blue flannel shirt. His gaze was piercing, as usual; they knew there was no reason to be afraid of him...but his few words and storm cloud eyes simply made them hesitate to approach him. He stood there, staring at them, pipe at the ready in his left hand. Suddenly, he gave one quick nod of the head and moved his eyes toward the waiting blacksmith.

Again, the kids looked at each other, widened their eyes, and stepped forward.

"So," Norma Jean began hesitantly to the blacksmith, "Have you ever built a cast iron stove?"

"Well, that's not the question I was expecting!" he laughed. "I have not. But, I might still be able to answer your question. What is it?"

Norma Jean continued, "If you were going to...going to..." She stopped and looked over at Howard and Gyp.

"If you were going to hide something on a cast iron stove, where'd ya do it?" Howard continued for her.

"What do you mean, 'hide something'?" the blacksmith asked bewildered.

"Okay, let's say...a key!" Gyp said. "Is there anyway you could...cast, I guess is the word...a key onto a cast iron stove?"

"Hmm...well the stove is made out of iron ore mixed with carbon. Then the hot molten mass is poured into sand casts and..." he looked at them. "But I don't think this is what you want to know." He picked up the bellows and forced a stream of air into the hot furnace. "I've gotta keep the fire going while I'm taking a break," he smiled.

Norma Jean could see they were getting nowhere with their question, so she said, "Imagine you wanted to hide a key to a treasure on a stove, where would you put it?"

"Ah, is this part of the treasure hunt game they've organized at the children's pavilion?" the muscular man asked.

The kids just looked at him, silent, not willing to lie, but hoping he'd believe his own question.

He laughed, "Okay then. Let's win this game. Let's see...if I was going to hide a key to a treasure box on a cast iron stove, I would..." he gazed around his shop, "I would put it in the chimney pipe damper."

"The chimney pipe damper?" Howard repeated.

"Yup. That's where I'd put it. There's a spring-loaded handle, made out of forged steel, sort of like a long pin, that goes right through the chimney pipe damper." He looked at them. They looked at him. "You have seen a cast iron stove, haven't you?" he asked.

"Yes," they all said together. And Norma Jean continued, "You mean that pin thing...that thing that you turn to let the smoke out of the flue...or to let less or more air into the stove...you mean that...key-like thing that opens and closes the damper!" she laughed.

"Hey! That's it!" the blacksmith also laughed. "I'd hide a key in the cast iron plate that turns the damper on the flue. I'd make the turning pin a key!"

"Thanks, Mister!" Howard said.

"You're welcome, kids," he said, standing up and putting his heavy apron back on. "That was a nice little break in my day." He picked up the bellows and forced some more air into the furnace. "*Au revoir!*" he said.

"*Au revoir!*" They repeated back to him, and waved.

The kids looked around for Grandad, but he was gone.

"I know exactly what he's talking about," Norma Jean said, excitedly.

"Well, so do we, Norma Jean," Howard squinted at her. "We've only used that key almost every day this summer!"

"How long do you think we have to stay here?" Norma Jean asked. "Let's go tell Dad we're ready to go home."

"Not yet, Norma Jean," Howard said, wandering towards the deep-fried beignets. "Dad gave me three dollars and I'm going to spend it."

They met up with the rest of the family late in the afternoon.

A makeshift band of musicians had started an improv band playing washboards stroked with bottle caps. They bought some chicory coffee and, together with new friends, they listened, tapping their toes. Gypsy danced a jig and Norma Jean joined him, not caring a whit about Howard's hoots of laughter.

Late that evening they started the caravan drive back home. Too tired to talk, they slept.

They were still sleeping when Mum knocked on the cabin door the next morning.

"Good morning, sleepyheads!" she said, opening the screen door. "I've brought you breakfast." She laid a plate of johnnycake along with honey-butter on the table.

"Far out, Mum!" Howard said. "Come on, guys! Get out of bed!"

Ten minutes later they were all seated with Mum around the table, eating and talking about their day.

Mum said, "Dad, the boys, Grandad, and Grandmum have already gone to the farm. We'll meet them there for morning coffee and then we've got to stay for the day to can the blueberries that Mère brought for me."

Norma Jean had noticed that Mum had been slipping the Cajun *Mère* into her speech lately. She liked it.

Mum continued, "And then Grandad has offered to bring you kids back to the lake."

Norma Jean, Howard, and Gyp looked at each other, then looked at the stove. "Great, Mum," was all that Norma Jean said.

Mum got up, "Meet me at the pickup truck in 15 minutes, okay?"

They all answered, *yes*, and as soon as she was gone, they rushed toward the stove. Howard reached up and turned the pin...no, the KEY...that was in the damper.

"Here it is; right here!" he said, jabbing the pin with his finger.

"Do you think Grandad is going to help us?" Norma Jean asked.

"It sure seems like it," Gyp responded.

Later that morning the family was having coffee on the farm house porch steps. The conversation was about harvest time fast approaching and the many things needed to be done and decisions that needed to be made: sharping the swather sickle; checking the moisture content of the wheat to determine which field needed harvesting first; guessing how many bushels to the acre could be expected; lessons from Dad on when and how to adjust the header on the combine to get the most wheat and the least straw; and the weather...everything depended on the weather...could they get finished harvesting before it rained, snowed, or, God forbid, hailed.

Norma Jean, Howard, and Gyp had been given the job of cutting the massive farmyard lawn and they were taking turns driving the four-speed, John Deere garden tractor. When it wasn't their turn, Norma Jean went inside to help with the canning, and Gyp and Howard went to the granaries to sweep out last year's wheat.

They waited anxiously for Grandad to honk the pickup's horn—the signal that they could head back to the lake.

Finally, they heard the blast. They came running, Nicky at their heels. Mum was holding Baby Barry on her hip, and was standing by the driver's door, talking to Grandad and Grandmum. When they saw the kids, Grandad jumped in the driver's side and Mum handed Baby Barry to Grandmum, went around to the other side of the truck, and jumped in beside him.

"Thanks for taking Barry for the afternoon, Mère," Mum said.

Grandmum smiled, kissed the top of his blonde head and said goodbye to Mum.

Norma Jean, Howard, and Gyp piled into the back, all three huddled on the floor of the truck-bed, beneath the back window and out of the wind. Nicky put his front paws onto the wheel well, at the ready for the warm wind.

They saw Dad wave from the machine shed, and they waved back.

"Here we go!" Norma Jean said excitedly. "I can hardly stand this!" She pointed to the box of tools that were at their feet. "Grandad can do anything, and he is definitely going to do SOMETHING to that stove."

They flew down the gravel road, at speeds only Grandad drove, turned onto the dirt laneway that wound through the hay field, past the small cabin... Mum yelled out her window, "We're going down to the lake to have a quick swim first. We're filthy!"

"OKAY!" the kids yelled back.

They took turns changing into their swimsuits in the boathouse. All except Grandad. He'd let everyone off and then driven back up the hill toward the cabin.

"Mum," Norma Jean finally had a chance to say, "What's going on?"

"I'm pretty sure you know," Mum winked. Then she ran down the pier, jumped in and started swimming. The kids followed her.

When they had all come up for air, Norma Jean continued, "Mum, is Grandad going to take the stove flue apart and see if the damper pin is a key?"

Howard had grabbed a big tractor inner-tube out of the boathouse and the kids pulled themselves up on it while Mum hung on to it.

"That's exactly what he's doing. Right now. He doesn't want you kids there yet," Mum said. "We'll go up in a bit. Let's just let Grandad work his magic. He's going to give two long blasts on the pickup truck's horn when he's finished."

Howard and Gyp started rocking the tube. "Ye-haw!" Howard shouted. "I KNEW we'd find it. I just KNEW it."

"We haven't found anything yet," Mum said. But she was smiling.

Mum got out of the water and went back into the boathouse to change. When she came out she sat on edge of the pier, watching them. Norma Jean watched her. *She's watching us, but she's not seeing us. Mum is every bit as excited as we are.* Norma Jean did a backflip off the tube and sent Howard and Gyp flying.

For the second time that day, they waited anxiously for the horn blast. Finally, it came: HONK HONK!

Out of the water they scrambled. Howard and Gyp stayed in their swim shorts and Norma Jean threw on a old cotton dress she used for a bathing suit cover-up. They quickly tied their runners and ran up the path to the cabins. Mum led the way, every bit as fast as the kids. Trotting down the dirt lane they entered the small yard of B.R.D.'s vintage home. Grandad was standing on the porch.

"Grandad!" Norma Jean panted, "Did you find it?"

He pulled an eight inch steel key from his overalls pocket. His black eyes twinkled and his mustache twitched.

Nicky barked; the coondog howled from the knoll; Hitchcock cawed from the spruce tree behind the outhouse; and a cow munched the new alfalfa that was already sprouting in the hay field.

Grandad put the key down on the table and without a word headed across the hayfield, taking the shortcut to Spruce Bay.

It was hard to sleep that night. Everyone was anxious to find the hole into which the key belonged.

Finally, Norma Jean said, "There's only one thing left to do," She went to the table and spread the notebook in front of her.

Clue Number 22: Grandad finds the key that was hidden in the stove.

Chapter 15
HOWARD USES HIS BIG THICK HEAD

Norma Jean, Howard, and Gypsy spent the rest of that day and all of the next wandering around the cabin, trying to fit the large key into every imaginable crevice. Nothing. They wanted desperately to believe that this was the key to the lost family treasure, but really, they had no way to know for sure.

It was late afternoon and they were sitting on the cabin porch steps, listening to Hitchcock caw from his perch on the peaked outhouse roof.

"What's next?" Howard asked dejectedly.

No one said anything.

Gyp went into the cabin and came back with the coffee pot that had been simmering on the stove.

He put it and three mugs onto the porch table and said, "I'm pouring. Who's drinking?"

Howard laughed. "I know where you heard that! The Acadian Day Festival. That guy was hilarious. Okay, Gyp...I'm drinking," he looked at Norma Jean, "and you don't have to tell Mum..."

"Sheesh, Howard, whaddaya think I am? I'm drinking too, Gyp. Give me the mug with Hiawatha on it. Maybe it'll inspire me."

"Inspire..." Howard started.

"How many sugars, Howard?" Gyp interrupted him. Now was not the time for sibling tit-for-tat.

"Load 'er up," Howard said.

"Me too," Norma Jean agreed. "Maybe some good ol' Cajun chicory coffee will..." she turned and looked Howard square in the eyes, "INSPIRE me."

Howard laughed again, and pretty soon Gyp and Norma Jean joined him.

"Why are we laughing, anyway?" Howard finally croaked.

"Who knows," Gyp said, "and it doesn't matter."

Howard and Norma Jean looked at each other and immediately both whispered, "It just doesn't matter."

"What?" Gyp asked.

They repeated it a little bit louder, "It Just Doesn't Matter."

"What doesn't matter?" Gyp asked again.

And then a little louder, "IT JUST DOESN'T MATTER."

By now Gyp got the gist of it and joined them.

They shouted it at the top of their lungs, "IT JUST DOESN'T MATTER!!!!!"

Nicky came barking up the steps and stood there wagging his tail as the mass of legs, arms, spilled coffee, and laughing tears encompassed the porch. They had learned this little ditty at camp last summer and until this moment had never thought to use it.

And then the coondog howled.

Norma Jean jumped up. "I know! It's time for a Western Red Cedar outing," she said.

"Now?" asked both Gyp and Howard, together.

"Of course now," she said, "Maybe the great-great-grand-mère has left us another clue. Come on," she said. Grabbing her knapsack, she jumped down all the stairs in one giant leap.

They raced each other down the dirt lane and were just about to pass the big cabin and start the twisting trail to the beach when Mum called, "Hey kids!"

"Oh shoot," Norma Jean said, "not the garden!" They turned back and Mum met them at the cabin door.

"No, not the garden," she laughed. "Bernard, you got a letter." She handed the envelope to Gyp. "I think it's from your folks," she smiled.

He took the letter, stuffed it in the back pocket of his cargo shorts, and turned to catch up with Howard and Norma Jean, who had kept running when they heard Mum say that it wasn't the garden. Best not stick around in case it was not the garden, but...the...chickens...or the...canning...or any number of other things Mum could come up with on a lovely summer afternoon.

They grabbed oars and lifejackets, kicked off their runners as they ran down the pier, jumped into the Western Red Cedar and cast off the bowline.

"Heave-ho!" Howard shouted as he pushed off. "Chart us a course, Norma Jean!" And they headed to the middle of the lake for their ritual deep water swim.

Soon Norma Jean called, "Swim-ho!" Shorts and T-shirts flew off to reveal bathing suits ready for action.

"Wait!" Norma Jean called, suddenly. "Gyp! You forgot to read your letter! In fact, you just about sent it overboard!" She grabbed his shorts, pulling them off the edge of the boat, and threw them at him.

"Oh man!" Gyp said, "Thanks!" He sat down on the middle seat and said, "Go ahead! I'll catch up with you in a minute."

"Cannonball!" Howard yelled as he curled into a ball and threw himself into the water.

"Swan-dive!" Norma Jean yelled as she gracefully fell from the port side.

Howard and Norma Jean barely had time to get their heads back above water when Gypsy started yelling and frantically waving his letter.

"Get out of the water, you two! Quick! We've got to go back to the cabin *de suite*! Right now!" He was getting the oars into the oar-locks as he spoke. Norma Jean and Howard didn't question him. Instead they somersaulted into the waiting Western Red and were on their way before you could say "Hitchcock". Howard quickly sat down beside Gyp and took an oar. The boys matched each other, pull for pull, and the boat left a wake to match the motor boat.

"What, Gyp? Tell us!" Norma Jean was sitting in the bow, facing the boys. Her suntanned face and blonde hair had feasted on summer sun and she was in her element.

"Here," Gyp said, handing the letter to Norma Jean, "Read this while Howard and I row."

Norma Jean took the letter, opened it up and read,

Dear Gypsy,
Here I am again, missing you like crazy...

"You can skip the first paragraph," Gypsy said, turning his face leeward. "Start where she says, 'Here's an interesting tidbit...'"

"*Here's an interesting tidbit about what the Acadian families did with their treasure when they had to flee...*"

Norma Jean stopped reading for a moment, and looked up at the boys.

"Read it!" Howard urged.

She continued: "*They buried it in the eastern section of the foundation of a church...*"

"That's enough!" Gyp shouted and looked at them, expectantly. "That's the clue we've been waiting for!"

Norma Jean and Howard looked at each other. Finally Norma Jean started, "Do you mean...?"

"YES!" Gypsy shouted, again. The treasure is buried in the eastern foundation of the cabin! I'm sure of it!"

"In the eastern foundation...?" Norma Jean asked.

"Yeah! Come on! Let's go!" Gyp turned his face toward the shore and dug the oar deep into the water.

The boys rowed as hard and fast as their growing muscles would allow. Norma Jean leaned over the bow, willing the boat to move faster.

"We need to think," she said. "The front porch is the eastern foundation. We can't dig up the whole porch. It's got to be more specific."

The boat moved along, the silence only broken by the plunging of the oars into the murky green algae lake water.

"I know!" Norma Jean said, suddenly. "*L'union fait la force,* Strength through Unity. We've got to find the Acadian foundation stone! That's got to be the clue that Mum's great-uncle left for her. It's got to be!"

Howard began to drag his oar and the boat turned a sharp right, toward the shore at Spruce Bay.

"What are you doing, Howard?" Gyp said, a hint of anxiety in his voice. "We've got to get back to the cabin!"

"How do we know that it's not the foundation stone that we found in the great- great-grand-mère's clearing?" he said.

The boys stopped rowing for a moment.

"You're right, Howard," Gyp said. "We don't know. It could be, but why would YOUR family treasure be buried on the Leblanc land?" He let his oar drop into the water and sighed. "This is stupid. I'm sorry. I just want you to find it so badly that I made more of Mom's letter than I should have." He slapped the oar on top of the water, watching the ripples head to shore. "Let's go swimming and forget the whole business." He stood up, rocking the boat, gently.

"Sit down!" Norma Jean said to him, sternly. "We need to THINK. Now...do it! THINK!" She put her knapsack on the wooden seat beside her and pulled out the notebook. "Let's go over everything we know, but first let me add this new one:

Clue Number 23: We think the treasure is hidden in an Acadian foundation stone."

For the next 10 minutes the kids read and reread the clues.

"You know," Howard said after they had exhausted all their *thinks*, "Remember when Mum told us that the cabin had burned down and been rebuilt?"

"Yeah. I forgot about that," Norma Jean said. "That makes the possibility of finding the foundation stone even more dismal."

"No it doesn't," Howard said. "You can use the same foundation stone to rebuild, but that's not my point."

He laid his oar keel to keel, crossed his arms on it and continued, "What if the great-great-grand-mère's foundation stone is a clue to OUR foundation stone?" He turned to Norma Jean, "Do you still have that compass that you grabbed from our fort?"

Norma Jean answered him by wordlessly pulling the compass out of her knapsack. She held it up so that it refracted sunlight and water, making them simultaneously squint. "Now what?" she asked, sensing that Howard was, once again, using that big overgrown head of his.

He put the oar back in the water, and Gyp followed suit. "Now, we go to great-great-grand-mères' and do some *deducing*." He smiled at Norma Jean. "I've got an idea."

They pulled the Western Red Cedar onto shore, no longer caring about who could see them. They ran to find the six trees that had originally unlocked the great-great-grand-mère's back door.

"Stop!" Howard demanded. Gyp and Norma Jean obeyed, looking at him. "Norma Jean, hand me your compass," he continued.

She pulled it out of her cut-offs' back pocket and handed it to him.

"Now," Howard continued, "Gyp, go and stand right on top of the foundation stone, right below the crescent moon."

Gyp ran to the tree, stood on the stone, turned back to face Howard and called, "Here!"

Howard stood in front of the first painted tree, looked at Gyp, and lined up the insignia with his eye. Then he looked down at the compass he was holding.

"Got it!" he called to Gyp. "You can come back now!"

Gyp came bounding back and both he and Norma Jean followed Howard, who was already getting back into the Western Red Cedar.

"Howard..." Gyp started, but Norma Jean interrupted him.

"Don't talk to him, Gyp. He might forget."

"I will not, Norma Jean," Howard said. "But just because you said that I'm not gonna tell you my idea." He laughed.

"It's probably stupid, anyway," she rolled her eyes at him. But she was smiling. And her eyes were shining. She knew Howard. And this was gonna be good.

They docked the boat, threw the oars and life jackets back in the boat house, and ran back up the steep, winding trail.

"Wait!" Norma Jean said just before they were within earshot of the big cabin. "Let's sneak past. Not a word, you two. If we get snagged for more chores, I'll... I'll blame you!"

Wordlessly and silently they slipped past the big cabin and ran back down the dirt lane to the cabin of mystery.

Nicky was laying across the top porch step and lifted his head as they approached. He whined softly but was back asleep as soon as Norma Jean whispered, "Good ol' boy," and rubbed his warm flank.

Howard ran to the outhouse and stood beneath the crescent moon. He looked down at the compass, did a quarter-turn and said, "Norma Jean come stand in front of me." She did so. He turned her around so that her back was to his face. "Now, start walking..." he looked at the compass and turned her a little more to the left, "Start walking..." he looked up, "and count six trees, but only the ones that touch your right arm."

Norma Jean slowly started walking. Her right hand brushed against a thick poplar tree. "ONE!" she shouted. She turned around and looked at Howard.

"Keep walking!" he said, his eye on the compass. "And Gyp, go get the coal shovel that's beside the stove!"

Gyp didn't say a word. He ran up the porch steps, slamming the screen door on the way in and again on the way out. This time Nicky got up, stretched, and came down the steps with Gyp. "Got it!" he called, waving the coal shovel frantically. He beelined for Norma Jean, who was still counting.

"SIX!" she yelled, and turned to face Howard. "Now what?" she called to him.

Howard ran to join her. The three of them stood there for moment, staring at each other. Then Howard smiled. "DIG!" he said, pointing at Norma Jean's feet.

She stepped aside and Gyp pushed the tip of the shovel into the hard, grassy soil. He put his foot on the top of the spade and jumped on it. The shovel went into the dirt four inches and...

"That's as far as it'll go!" Gyp said, his eyes wide and his grin wider.

"Pretend you're digging potatoes, Gyp!" Howard encouraged him.

"I've never dug potatoes!" Gyp laughed, but still he slid the tip of the shovel horizontally and lifted the top layer of dirt.

Nicky, caught up in the excitement, muzzled his way through the crowd and began pawing the ground where Gyp had lifted the dirt.

"Atta boy, Nicky!" Howard laughed. "You do the work. Who needs a shovel when ya gotta dirt-digging black lab?"

Gyp and Nicky took turns digging. Then all three kids got down on their hands and knees and unearthed what was, unmistakably, a metal box.

Chapter 16
TRICKSTERS

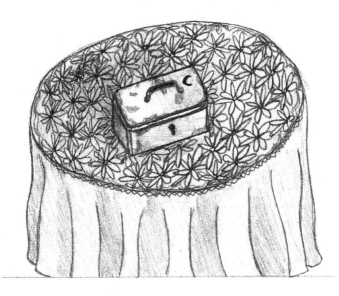

The box sat, in all its glory, in the middle of the kitchen table. They had brushed and whittled the years and years of dirt off it, found the side handles and carried it to the small cabin...back to its ancestral home, at least its western Canadian home. Where it had been before being brought West was anyone's guess.

They sat there looking at it for much of the afternoon. Now that they had actually found a *treasure box* they hesitated to open it. Somehow it felt church-like. It needed to be given respect. They talked softly, almost whispering, about what to do now.

"Do you think the key fits it?" Howard asked.

"Absolutely," Norma Jean answered. "You can tell just by looking at it."

They continued to stare at it, sometimes walking around the table where it sat, circling it like a hunter in awe of his prey.

"What should we do?" Howard looked at the other two, finally asking the question that lay heavy in the room.

Gyp got up and poked at the banked fire. "I'm making some coffee," he said.

They sat at the table, steaming mugs of chicory coffee in front of them and continued to stare at the old, dirty, metal box.

"It's odd, isn't it, that we're hesitating to open it?" Norma Jean mused.

Neither Gyp nor Howard answered her. It was one of those questions that just needed to be asked, not answered. *Rhetorical*, Norma Jean remembered the term but didn't say it out loud.

They sat for the next hour, afternoon coffee in hand, chatting about the summer and when they'd have to say goodbye to Gyp and go back to school. They made plans for how they'd see each other again, and the things they'd do in future summers.

Finally they heard the whine of the changing gears on the pickup truck.

"That's Dad," Howard said, jumping up and heading toward the porch. "The boys will be right behind him." He had barely finished his sentence when they heard Allan beep his horn as he drove his brand new (to him) Chevrolet pickup past the small cabin, heading to the big cabin for supper.

"Man, it's supper time," Howard said, waving to the boys as they drove by. "Let's go! We can talk to Mum and Dad about what to do."

Norma Jean hesitated. "I guess...but what about the boys? Will they do something...stupid?"

"Norma Jean, just because we're boys doesn't mean we're *stupid*. Who found the treasure box?"

Norma Jean looked at him.

"Who, Norma Jean?!" Howard raised his voice and laughed.

"OK!" Norma Jean gave Howard a playful push down the porch steps. "Let's go, then! We'll all talk about it at supper."

"Sure, but WHO, Norma Jean?!" Howard picked her up and threw her across his left shoulder. "Who?!"

Norma Jean screamed, "YOU! YOU!! YOU!!! You big idiot! Now put me down!"

Howard placed her back on terra-firma and banged his chest like Tarzan, yelling as he did so:

"ME! TARZAN! YOU! NOT JANE!"

Gyp laughed and started running up the dirt lane, "Come on, you...nitwits!"

Norma Jean caught up with him and said, "NITWITS? You've been with us too long, Gyp."
She gave him a shove and they all ran full-speed ahead, toward the chili and johnnycake.

The whole family was seated around the big kitchen table. The lake cabin had so much more room than the farm house, and the space always made supper at the lake feel like a holiday. There were no set places and the free-for-all seating was loud and physical. When everyone was seated, Norma Jean stood up and said,

"Be quiet everyone! I have something to say!"

Dad raised his eyebrows, looked at Norma Jean and grinned.

"Sit down, Norma Jean!" Les yelled. "I wanna eat..."

Norma Jean looked at Dad. He put his knife and fork down and looked at Les. "Hang on there, Les. You can still eat while Norma Jean talks. Don't let that slow you down. Now, what is it, Norma Jean?"

Everyone became quiet and looked at her. She looked around the table and stopped her gaze at Howard. "Actually, Howard has something to say." Norma Jean sat down. "Tell them, Howard."

"Do I have to stand?" Howard asked.

"No, you goofball," Norma Jean said. "But TELL them!"

Howard took a bite of johnnycake with honey-butter and waited just long enough for Norma Jean to give him a swat, then laughed and said to the listening family, "Okay. We found the treasure box. It was buried beside the small cabin."

Everyone stopped eating, even Les.

Mum stood up. "What's in it?" she asked, the excitement vivid in her voice.

"We haven't opened it yet," Howard continued. "We just thought we should wait... for... I don't know. We just thought we should wait."

"That was the right thing to do. Grand-père and Grand-mère should be here," Mum said. Again, Norma Jean noticed that mum was calling her parents by their Cajun names. "Andy, I've got to go to Spruce Bay right now and use the pay phone." Mum went to a syrup can on the pantry shelf, pulled out some coins, and walked out the door, headed to the trail that led to the lake and the neighbouring resort.

"Wait! Mum! I'm coming with you!" Norma Jean said and ran to catch up.

"Me, too!" Gyp called and was close on the heels of Norma Jean.

Howard looked at them, looked at his still full bowl of chili, and looked at Kathy. She laughed, "Don't worry. I'll save it for you," she said. And Howard was off.

They all ran, even Mum, her apron strings streaming behind her like a school-girl's braids.

The campfires were blazing and supper was cooking at the dozen or so campsites they flew past. The summer evening sun was still high and the motor boats buzzed and skimmed the murky lake, as if anxious to get the last waterskier pulled before fall came.

The fishermen had moved their crafts into the reeds and sat camouflaged and determined to catch yet another lake trout and to get it into the deep-freezer before the weather made them switch from rowboat fishing to ice-hut fishing.

The small camp store and café was still open, assuring the campers that they could still buy briquets that had been forgotten at home, or milk for the children, or a chocolate bar for dessert.

Dixie was behind the counter, talking to a young man who was perched on a café stool and drinking a bottle of orange pop through a straw. She moved away from him when she saw the three Nielsens and Gypsy running toward her.

"Hey! What's going on?" she asked, the concern evident in her voice.

"We're fine, Dixie!" Mum panted and smiled. "We must look like a herd of wild horses, though!" she laughed. "I'm just here to use the pay phone, and the kids joined me. Dixie, if I send someone down with the money tomorrow, will you give these kids a pop, please?"

"You know I will, Mrs. Nielsen. Are the boys coming too?" Dixie asked, glancing at the teenager sitting on the stool.

"No." Mum said. "I believe they're all still eating chili and johnnycake at the cabin."

Norma Jean watched Dixie with interest. There was such an air of teenage mystery in this girl with the tight sleeveless sweaters and short hot-pants. Tonight Dixie was wearing black eyeliner and blue eyeshadow. Norma Jean had been wanting to buy some at Kressges but she knew Mum wouldn't let her. Looking like Dixie would never be her goal, but still, she wanted to try that eyeshadow. Yes, Dixie was of great interest to Norma Jean. But tonight, Dixie was going to give her a pop, and she wanted that more than eyeshadow.

Howard chose Mountain Dew, Gyp, Coke, and Norma Jean, Grape Crush. "Thanks!" they chorused together and popped the caps off. They sat on three of the four café counter stools.

Norma Jean looked at the young man beside her. He looked at her and then swung his glance back to Dixie. "I'll see you later, Dixie." He stood up, looked out at the lake, took his comb out of his back pocket and ran it through his greasy hair, then sauntered off towards the campsites.

Dixie sighed and said, "The store closes at 10PM, Paddy. Maybe I'll see ya then?"

Paddy didn't turn around. Norma Jean and Dixie both watched him as he walked away. In his tight Levis and black tee shirt he could have been one of Norma Jean's brothers. But he wasn't and that's why she watched him. Norma Jean looked back at Dixie and saw that she was watching her. Dixie smiled at her and Norma Jean smiled back. Suddenly Gypsy seemed like a kid.

Mum was putting coins into the pay phone and the kids all turned their attention there, even Dixie. They waited several seconds while the call went through; finally Mum said, "Mère?"

There were a few more seconds of silence and then Mum continued, "Mère, you and Père must come back." Again, a few seconds of silence. "Yes, Andy could always use help and I'd love another batch of peaches, but Mère...the kids have found the treasure box!"

Dixie gasped and looked to her left, into the side room off the café. Her Grand-père came out and crossed his massive arms on the counter, leaning over to look at Mum, who was huddled in the corner of the porch, phone to her ear.

"No, they haven't opened it yet," Mum continued, "and I don't think they should until you get here. Can you come?" And again, Mum was silent.

Norma Jean looked at the Grand-père. His red and blue checked cotton shirt was rolled up at the sleeves. She stared at his right forearm. There in fading blues, yellows, reds, and oranges, was the Acadian insignia.

Howard was sitting between her and Gyp and he started to kick them both. He had seen it too. Gyp casually glanced over at them, eyes wide and then followed Norma Jean's eye-movement directive. Gyp took a sip of pop and glanced over at the Grand-père. All three of them looked at each other for a second and then turned their attention back to Mum.

"Thank you, Mère. We'll plan a big lake party when you get here. Can you bring Marie and Donna?" A moment's pause... "See you then. Bye!"

Mum turned to speak to the kids, and then saw the Grand-père and Dixie. She was silent for just a moment, then she smiled. "They're coming. And they're bringing your aunts," she said, looking at the kids.

"Hooray!" Howard shouted. "And can we have steak at the party?"

"No," Mum said and laughed. "We're gonna roast a pig!" She turned to the grand-père and Dixie, "And you're all invited! Come on Saturday at five PM. And...please bring the great-great-grand-mère."

Grand-père smiled and said, "*L'union fait la force.*"

"Strength through Unity," Norma Jean whispered and the grand-père looked at her and smiled even bigger.

"Don't worry about the pops, Mrs. Nielsen," Dixie said. "They're on the house. This Acadian house. *Très bien.*"

"Thanks, Dixie," Mum said. "See you Saturday." She put her hands into her apron pockets and walked off the porch, back to the trailhead and the cabin. The kids followed close behind until they could take the slow pace no longer and raced ahead of Mum, all the way back to the big cabin.

Kathy had, true to her word, saved Howard's supper, and had added Gyp and Norma Jean's to the warming oven, also. The three of them sat back down at the table, listening as the boys got ready for their evening ski. Within a half hour everyone was back down at the lake, taking the final swim, ski, and boat ride before the sun set completely.

It had been a very, very full day, and by the time Norma Jean, Howard, and Gyp were walking down the dirt lane toward the small cabin, the lake had quieted and the lights from the massive starry host had begun to dance in the black sky. The kids sat on the porch steps, talking about the events of the day, and how hard it would be to wait five days for Saturday to come, and how Gyp would be going home to Lafayette next week, and when would they see each other again...but most of all they talked about what was in the treasure box.

They were all starting to yawn and breathe a little slower when Nicky came and joined them, laying down at their feet, thumping his tail on the packed dirt.

Howard reached down and patted his belly, "Where you been all day, boy? We've had all kinds of stuff going on today."

Just then the coondog let out a loud, long howl. The kids looked toward the knoll where they had first spotted the great-great-grand-mère and the dog standing. There she was again, silhouetted against the night sky, and her coondog with face raised to the moon, howling.

Suddenly Howard jumped up. "I have a bad feeling..." he ran into the cabin, letting the screen door slam behind him. "I knew it!" He yelled. "It's gone! The treasure box is gone!"

He was back on the porch in seconds, colliding with Norma Jean and Gyp, who had raced toward the door.

"What!!" Norma Jean asked, incredulous.

"It can't be!" Gyp croaked.

"Quick! Someone light the lantern!" Norma Jean demanded as she searched for the flashlight.

Howard pumped the kerosene lamp while Gyp lit the match. The silk bags flared with light as the oil and fire met. Howard held the lantern high and the kids frantically searched the small cabin. Finally, he said, "Norma Jean, get out the notebook at write:

Clue Number 24: Treasure found; treasure lost."

There was no mistaking it. The treasure box, which had been so carefully placed on the table in the middle of the room, was gone.

Chapter 17
NORMA JEAN'S REVENGE

Norma Jean looked out the cabin door to see if the lights were still on in the big cabin. Everything was dark. The family had gone to bed. After discussing it around the table, the kids decided not to wake Mum and Dad. They knew that Dad worked hard and sleep was important to him. Nothing could be done in the dark, anyway.

Finally, they went to bed, but no one slept until the wee hours of the morning. Hitchcock had come back and was cawing up a storm right outside the window by Norma Jean's bed.

"I hate that blackbird," Norma Jean said, rolling over and covering her ears with her blankets.

She heard the cabin door open and close, softly. She sat up and looked out the window. Gyp, dressed in only his PJ bottoms, had come around the backside of the cabin and stood underneath the spruce tree where Hitchcock was perched. Norma Jean faintly heard his voice but the words were unintelligible—she knew French classes were in her future and never before this summer had she wanted to bother with them. Now, she couldn't wait. Hitchcock and Gyp stared at one another for a moment, then with one long caw the blackbird flew away.

Gyp came back inside and climbed into his bed. "You're welcome," he said.

Norma Jean smiled to herself. *Now, THAT'S not something a brother would do*.

The kids woke late the next morning and took their time getting breakfast. They didn't bother with the fire and coffee. They had their bread untoasted, with peanut butter and fresh peach jam. Sitting on the porch steps they finally brought up the topic that was foremost on their minds: the missing treasure box.

"So...what should we do?" Howard asked.

Silence.

They heard Nicky barking and could see him across the hayfield. Howard stood up and called, "NICKY! COME 'ERE, BOY!" The dog let loose of the gopher he was playing with and bounded towards the kids.

All three of them jumped up and ran to the panting dog as he stood at the bottom of the porch steps. Around his belly was a string and attached to the string was, unmistakably, a note.

Howard rubbed Nicky's head to make him hold still, while Norma Jean ran into the cabin to get a knife to cut the binder twine. Gyp just stood there, saying over and over again, "*Oh mon Dieu, oh mon Dieu.*"

"Whatcha got here, Nicky?" Howard said, as Norma Jean cut the string. "You bringing us a note from that ol' coondog?"

Norma Jean pulled a piece of white tee-shirt fabric off the binder twine and hastily laid it out on the already warm porch steps.

"Read it!" Howard urged as he let Nicky go. "What's it say, Norma Jean?"

"Great jumpin' St. Afan, Norma Jean, hurry!" Gyp joined in.

They all huddled around the note and Norma Jean read it aloud, "*The summer's not over; find the four-leaf clover.*"

They all looked at each other. Then Norma Jean picked the note up, stuffed it in her cut-offs back pocket, put her hands on her hips and yelled at the top of her lungs, "I HATE THOSE STUPID BOYS!"

Gyp and Howard looked at her and then at each other.

"They'd really do that?" Gyp said.

"Yes, they'd really do that," Norma Jean said, "because they're STUPID!"

She took off, running up the lane to the big cabin. Gyp and Howard just let her go. Their own disappointment seemed dwarfed by Norma Jean's anger and they decided to go ahead and unbank the fire to make some coffee. Howard had been steadily drinking it again, Nick's Brew gone by the wayside, but two tablespoons of sugar added instead made it *sweeter than love*. And at age ten, that was fine with him.

The two boys were sitting on the porch steps, still drinking coffee, when they could see Norma Jean coming back down the lane, carrying something. They got up and ran to meet her.

"You found it, already?" Gyp asked.

"Yes. Their clues are even stupider than they are," Norma Jean said.

Howard kept silent. He was also angry at the boys and wanted Norma Jean to vent as much as possible before she remembered that he was also *a boy*. Today, he was glad he wasn't one of *the boys*. Norma Jean would not soon forget this trick. He smiled in spite of himself. Whatever she was going to do...it would be good.

"I read the stupid clue to Mum," Norma Jean continued, "And she found the treasure box immediately, under a stupid quilt that had a stupid four-leaf clover on it. They are so stupid they couldn't even hide it well. It took Mum and me 30 seconds to figure it out."

Howard was not going to say that it sounded like Mum figured it out. No, he would not say anything stupid right now. He was not going to be one of the stupid boys today.

"Mum said I could go ahead and bring it back here and it would be perfectly safe until Saturday. She'll give those stupid boys..."

"...*l'enfer*," Gyp filled in for her.

Once again, Norma Jean couldn't wait for grade six French to start in the fall. "Yup, she'll give 'em *l'enfer*. And I wanna be there to hear it, the stupid heads."

By now she thought she had repeated "stupid" as many times as she'd needed to in order to appease her anger, and she was ready to join the boys in a cup of chicory coffee.

"Wait," she said first, going into the cabin and grabbing the notebook, "I need to say 'stupid' one more time. Clue Number 25: The boys are STUPID." She slammed it shut, glaring at Gyp and Howard. They wisely kept their mouths shut.

"Okay, let's talk about our day," she said after she put the notebook away and was sitting on the porch steps, coffee in one hand and treasure box in the other.

***

Three days later Grand-père and Grand-mère (they had all started to call them that) drove through the hayfield and parked a shiny new Airstream travel trailer beside the big cabin. The aunties were with

218

them and the noise of reunion echoed from one side of the lake to the other.

Ever since the treasure box had gone missing (and found) the kids had not even so much as hinted to the boys that anything had happened. Mum and Dad had also both agreed to keep silent. As far as the boys knew, the box was still missing and no one had noticed! Norma Jean, Howard, and Gyp were loving watching the boys watch them. Every now and then Norma Jean saw them whispering together. It was very, very satisfying.

The preparations for the party continued as Dad brought shovels from the farm, and on Friday evening he and Grand-père started digging the pit for the pig that was to be roasted the next day. They dug it three-feet deep, and six-feet by four-feet wide. The boys brought rocks up from the lakeshore to line the pit, and chopped up several downed and dried pine trees they found on the edge of the property. The wood fuel for the pit was ready. Howard collected kindling and together they started the fire in the bottom of the pit. Dad, Grand-père, and the boys each took a turn stoking and building it up.

By morning, there was a coalbed one-foot deep, ready for the 75 pound suckling pig that was being prepared by the butcher. The pig was delivered early Saturday morning and everyone was there to watch as the dressed pig was rolled in foil, then a clean, wet gunny sack, and finally wrapped in chicken wire. But before any of that was done, Dad had handed Norma Jean a big, red apple and opened the pig's jaws so she could put it in its mouth.

"To keep the oxygen flowing through the cavity," Dad said, when Norma Jean asked him why.

The coals were pushed to the side and Dad and Grand-père lowered the pig into the hot oven. A metal sheet was placed over the pig and dirt piled on top of it.

"Now," Dad said, looking around the group, "We go swath that northwest quarter of the Pixley place." Dad continued to give the boys their orders for the day, while Norma Jean, Howard, and Gyp joined the Aunties for breakfast in the travel trailer. Grand-père went with the men to the farm, and Mum, Kathy, and Grand-mère started to make peach pies for the evening festivities.

Midmorning Bedstefar dropped Bedstemor at the lake before he went to the farm, and she immediately joined in both the visiting and the meal preparation by peeling and coring apples for applesauce and telling the aunties the best cream sauce recipe for the peas they were shelling. Kathy was peeling potatoes for salad and all the women were drinking hot coffee with the rich cream that Bedstemor brought. She had skimmed it off the fresh milk that was delivered to their home every day and brought it to share with the family.

The kids swam, rowed, and ran the trails all day. In the late afternoon when the men came from the farm, the boat started up and everyone skied, even Mum.

Dixie and her Grand-père had walked the trail over to the Nielsen lakefront property, a huge tupperware bowl of coleslaw in hand. Norma Jean didn't know where Dixie's mum and dad were and when she had asked about it, Mum had just said, "Never mind anything but your own mind." And that was that.

It felt like Christmas. The whole family there, waiting...waiting...waiting for the big event: the opening of the gifts. But this time it was the opening of the treasure box. It felt like the moment would never come. But, finally, it did. Norma Jean had convinced Dad and Mum to open the box before they ate.

Makeshift sawhorse and plywood tables, covered with brightly coloured cloths were neatly arranged off the west side of the big cabin. The pig had been dug out of the pit and the aroma of the waiting meat filled the air. The sun was just starting to consider setting but wasn't in a hurry. And on the knoll, sat the great-great-grand-mère and her coondog. Both had refused to come but wanted their presence known. And so they gathered...Norma Jean, Howard, Gypsy, the boys, Kathy, baby Barry, Mum, Dad, Grand-père, Grand-mère, the two aunties, Bedstefar, Bedstemor, Dixie, and her Grand-père...18 folks, waiting for the opening of the treasure box.

"Well, everyone, this is a big day," Dad began. "I know we've all been looking forward to the opening of the Acadian family treasure box, but..." he paused as Mum walked over to him and took his hand. He continued quietly, "It's gone missing."

"No!" Grand-mère got out of her lawn chair.

Norma Jean let out a gasp. "But Dad!" she said, "I thought...!"

Dad interrupted her, "I'm sorry, Norma Jean. I can't even tell you how sorry I am...sorry for all of you." He reached around Mum and hugged her.

Howard cried out, "But Dad! I heard you on the phone with the police. I thought they'd found out who..."

"It's true, Howard. They think they have found the culprit and will let me know as soon as they pick him up. Hopefully, it will be soon and hopefully the treasure box is safe."

"But..." Keith started and then stopped and looked at his brothers. They shrugged at him.

Dad turned to look at the big boys, "The kids told Mum and me about the stolen box a few days ago. We had thought the box would be safe with them in the small cabin but we misjudged the security of this lake community. Obviously, the word got out that we had found the treasure, and...well, someone came into the small cabin and stole the box."

"I can't believe someone would do that!" Grand-mère said and started to weep quietly. The aunties went to her, wrapped their arms around her and said, "Go ahead, Mère...cry all you want. It's heartbreaking."

Grand-père turned and walked ten paces into the hayfield and stood with his back to the family, hands in this overall pockets.

Dixie started to shriek dramatically, "No! Please, no! This will kill Great-great-grand-mère." She fell into her Grand-père's arms sobbing hysterically.

Bedstefar and Bedstemor started whispering together in Danish, tut-tutting, and shaking their heads.

"So, Dad," Norma Jean said, "the cops really have a lead?"

"Yes, and as I said I'd hoped to hear from them before I made this terrible announcement, Norma Jean," Dad sighed and looked at her. "I've been waiting all day. They were going to let me know as soon as they picked the culprit up."

Gyp said, "I'm sorry, everyone. It's all my fault. I'm the one who wanted to keep it in the small cabin. It's all my stupid fault." He looked to be on the verge of tears.

Howard stood beside him, and gently laid his hand upon his shoulder, "No it ain't, Gyp. We told you the cabin was safe. We thought it was, really we did."

Norma Jean glanced carefully toward the boys. They were shifting uncomfortably. She stifled her smile while savouring the moment.

"Now, come on," Les said, "It must be somewhere."

"Yeah," Allan continued, "Have you looked...everywhere?"

"Like inside the big cabin?" Keith added. He started to walk toward it.

"We've searched and searched," Dad said. "It's simply gone."

Keith stopped walking. The boys all looked at each other, worry evident on their brows.

At that moment, a siren was heard, and a Royal Canadian Mounted Police (R.C.M.P.) car drove down the dirt lane, through the hayfield, and stopped in front of Grand-père. The Mountie rolled his window down and talked to him for a moment. They both looked over at the family, and Grand-père pointed towards the three older boys. "That's them, right there!" Everyone heard him say.

The Mountie got out of the car. "Hi, Andy," he said. "These your boys?"

"You know they are, Ralph. What's this all about?" Dad said, walking toward the uniformed man. The Mountie approached the boys. Mum came up behind her sons and stood with them.

"I have ONE question to ask you boys," the policeman said.

Dad came and stood beside the officer, staring at the boys and Mum.

The boys looked around the group, fear in their eyes.

"Boys..." the man said, "Would you play on the Hill End community baseball team?"

The boys looked at him in stunned silence and then the whole family broke into laughter. And they laughed, and they laughed, and they laughed. Every single one of them.

"Thanks, Ralph!" Dad said. "That was perfect! You had those boys ready to confess to the kidnaping of the Queen! Now, come on! Stay and eat with us."

"You wouldn't be able to stop me, Andy! How long have you been roasting this pig?" Ralph bent over the table where the platters of pork were laying and took a big sniff. "Man, I'm gonna eat my weight in this before the sun sets."

"Go on and get the treasure box, Norma Jean!" Dad called. "And..." he winked at Norma Jean, "good one, Yommpy-Doodle-Dandy!" He looked at his sons, slapped them on their backs and laughed some more. "So, boys! Ya wanna play on that baseball team? Ralph ain't leavin' until he gets your statement!"

Norma Jean winked back at Dad. "On it!" Norma Jean said. Then she looked straight at the boys, "Because summer isn't over and I'm holding the lucky four-leaf clover!" The family burst out laughing again.

"All right, all right!" Allan said. "You got us!"

"Yeah," Keith said, "You got us good."

"Weirdo," Les said, looking at Norma Jean, but he smiled sheepishly.

Norma Jean ran to the big cabin and pulled the box from the bottom shelf of the cupboard where Mum had been hiding it. Now the big moment really was here. Her stomach felt a little upset with all the excitement. Roast pig and coleslaw were not the first thing on Norma Jean's mind right now. Her Acadian family history lay in this dirty box that she was placing on the sawhorse table. She put the box down and grabbed Mum's hand.

"Note to self," she said under her breath, "<u>Clue Number 26</u>: It's very satisfying to trick your older brothers." She knew that Howard and Gyp might make her take this clue out, but she didn't care. She just needed to say it.

Chapter 18
L'UNION FAIT LA FORCE

"Drum roll and key, please," Dad said. He held out his palm to Norma Jean.

Panicked, she looked at Howard and Gyp. They laughed and Gyp pulled out the chain from around his neck to which he had added the stovepipe key. Norma Jean had been so intent on setting up the trick that she had totally lost track of who was looking after the key. She sighed in relief and Gyp brought the key to Dad.

Ralph went over to his cruiser, turned on the red and blue lights and blasted the siren for ten seconds. "There ya go, Andy! A good ol' Pine Lake drum roll!"

The coondog howled and everyone laughed. The great-great-grand-mère was still sitting on the knoll, faithful dog by her side. "That coondog deserves some of this roasted pork!" Dixie said. She looked at her Grand-père who nodded his head, smiling.

"I can't stand it another minute, Dad," Norma Jean said, "Open the box!!"

Dad took the key and slowly fitted it into the bottle-cap sized lock on the side of the old tin box. It turned with difficulty, but it turned. He looked at Norma Jean, "You do it, Norma Jean. Open the lid."

Norma Jean looked at Howard who nodded slightly. "No," she said, "Gypsy, YOU open it. We never would have known about Cajun family treasure if you hadn't come. Please. You open the box."

Gyp moved forward, as did the rest of the family. He carefully lifted the dirt-encrusted lid.

Dad looked at Norma Jean, winked again, and said, "Grand-mère, you come and take out the first item." Norma Jean smiled her agreement.

Grand-mère stepped in front of the box and lifted out a French Bible. "Look!" she said, opening the first page. Then she read aloud:

My dear Marie,
You are the order to my past;
You are the joy of my present;
You are the hope for my future.
The key to future happiness
is remembering your past.
If you do not, the key is not for you,
but for another.
Love, Père

Norma Jean looked at Grand-mère and saw not an older-than-middle-age woman who ran a roadside café, but a strong frontier woman whose ancestors had looked the English army in the eye and said, *Never will we bow to your King and never will we give up our faith!* And they had buried their treasures in the foundations of their homes and fled for their very lives.

The whole family had grown strangely quiet.

Grand-mère took the key that Dad had set on the table, held it aloft and said, "Whatever we find in this box has been left to us, but our Acadian blood has already been given to us." She took her time, looking each family member in the eye, "The future is ours and the key to future happiness lies in remembering where we came from. We are Acadian!"

"*L'union fait la force!*" Dixie's Grand-père suddenly shouted, throwing a fist in the air.

"Strength through Unity!" Norma Jean, Howard, and Gyp shouted in return, surprising everyone around them.

Bedstefar and Bedstemor nodded solemnly. The old country was never far from their thoughts.

Grand-mère put the Bible down and stepped away from the table.

"Wait, Grand-mère," Norma Jean said, a little bit too loudly. Howard and Gyp looked at her. She continued, "Is there anything else in the Bible?" She shrugged at them. Maybe it was silly but she just had a feeling...she looked at Howard and Gyp and then looked at the sky. Hitchcock was circling, cawing his fool head off. It just seemed... "Could you look, Grand-mère?" she asked timidly.

"There's lots in the pages of the Bible, Norma Jean," Dad laughed.

Norma Jean heard Allan whisper under his breath, "Yeah, but not *thou shalt not listen to rock music*." She pretended she didn't hear him.

"You know what I mean, Dad," she turned to Grand-mère, "Just look through the pages, Grand-mère...see if there's anything else. Any more notes?"

Grand-mère went back to the table and carefully leafed through the pages of the Bible. She stopped suddenly and looked up at Norma Jean. "You're right! There's another paper here."

"What's it say, Grand-mère?" Norma Jean was standing beside her, trying to look over her shoulder.

"You read it, Norma Jean," Grand-mère said, handing the worn linen paper to her.

"Okay, thanks, Grand-mère," Norma Jean said. She took the paper and carefully spread it on the sawhorse table. Howard and Gyp crowded around her.

"What are you thinking, Norma Jean?" Howard whispered.

"I think it has something to do with the Leblancs!" she whispered back. "Haven't you ever wondered why our great-great...how many greats I don't know...uncle had to hide our family's Acadian treasure and the clue to finding it was hidden on the Leblanc land?"

Dad came and joined the huddle, "Everyone's waiting, kids. Is there a problem?"

"No," Norma Jean said. "We're just trying to figure something out." She looked at Howard and Gyp and whispered, "I'm gonna read it out loud and what it is, it is."

Norma Jean straightened up, cleared her throat, and read out loud, "A message to my future Acadian family: Because you are reading this letter, I know that the solemn Acadian pact I have made with the Leblanc family has been honoured." Norma Jean looked up and saw that Dixie and her Grand-père had stepped closer and were staring at her. She continued, "My dear family has died, all of them. I have no one left in in this desolate Western Frontier. There is no one to whom I may leave this box of treasures. And so, I bury it, hoping that future generations will not forget their past and will find the signs and clues I have left hidden in this small cabin and on the Leblanc land."

Norma Jean heard Dixie's Grand-père gasp. "So there IS gris-gris," he whispered. He looked over at the great-great-grand-mère who was standing, her face to the heavens. The coondog raised his head and howled, long and loud.

"There's more," Norma Jean said, afraid of breaking the spell. She continued, "This treasure box will only be found by one who has looked to their *past,* finds joy in their *present,* and who feels hope for their *future.* You, dear Soul, are a worthy Acadian. Never forget there is *L'union fait la force.*"

"Strength through Unity," the family spontaneously translated the French to English.

"In this box are the treasures our family fled with during *Le Grand Dérangement*. Many died but our spirit has carried on. It is now in you."

Norma Jean put the letter down and looked at Grand-mère. "This box is for you, Grand-mère," she said.

"No, Norma Jean," Grand-mère replied, "This box is for us." She looked at Dixie and Grand-père Leblanc, "for all Acadian souls whose blood stained the foundation stones of their homeland."

They were all silent for a moment until Dad said, "There's still more things in the box. Florence? Your turn."

Mum stepped forward, looked at Mère, who smiled at her, and then she put her hand into the box, pulling out yet another piece of paper. "This is old!" she said. "It's like fabric or something. Certainly not like the paper we write on today."

"What is it, Mum?" Norma Jean couldn't help herself.

Mum slowly unfolded the paper. "It's...it's..." she handed it to Gyp. "It's French! What does it say, Bernard?"

Gyp took the paper, studied it for a moment and began to sing, "Jambalaya, crawfish pie, filé gumbo," he laughed as Allan joined him, "For tonight I'm a gonna meet my..."

Allan caught Dad's eye and stopped singing. "So, what is it Gyp?" Allan said.

"It's a recipe for jambalaya!" Gyp said.

"Let me see!" Grand-mère held out her hand and Gyp placed the brown and tattered fabric-like paper into it. "Well, what do you know. It's a family recipe! The Hiawatha café just got a new menu item."

"Sounds good to me!" Howard said and everyone laughed.

"This is fun, Dad! Who gets to dip into the treasure box next?" Norma Jean was practically jumping up and down.

Dad looked around the sober but happy group. "How 'bout Kathy. Step up to the box of treasure, Kathy!"

Everyone clapped and Kathy dipped into the box and pulled out a cowbell. She rang it loudly, laughing as she did so. Nicky barked his approval. "Why is there a cowbell in our Acadian family treasure box?" she said.

And again the coondog howled. Everyone was silent for a moment as they looked toward the knoll and the pair that were sitting in the growing twilight.

"It's the gris-gris," Mum said. "The cowbell is part of the Cajun gris-gris. It's an omen for good things to come." She smiled at Grand-mère. "Things like jambayla at the Hiawatha café."

"Hear! Hear!" Howard yelled, and Nicky started barking. Again, everyone laughed.

"Okay, Norma Jean," Dad said. "You're next in line; step up to the table."

Norma Jean felt her stomach do a turn and a chill form on the base of her neck. She closed her eyes, reached in the box and felt around. Her fingers gripped a small leather-bound book. She pulled it out, "It's...it's a..." she carefully opened it up. "It's a notebook!"

"A notebook!" Mum laughed. "Who knew that you came from a long line of notebook keepers, Norma Jean!"

She read the first page: "*Dear   Diary*...oh Mum! It's a diary!"

"Whose?" Mum asked, "Whose diary?" Mum was every bit as excited as Norma Jean.

Norma Jean slowly turned the page and saw the signature, "Marie! Oh my goodness this is Marie's diary!!" Norma Jean was practically hysterical with joy and surprise.

"What's the big deal?" Les said but Mum quickly shushed him.

"Howard?" Dad said, looking in the tin box, "There's something in here that you and Gyp might find interesting." He looked at the big boys, "You too, boys. Come and have a look."

The boys all approached the table and looked in the box.

Slowly, Dad lifted a small, black cast iron kettle out of the heavy tin box.

"A kettle?" Les asked, looking quizzically at Dad.

"My guess is that this kettle isn't meant for family tea time." Dad winked at Mum who in turn looked at Grand-père.

He picked up her cue and said, "If Cajun tradition has followed this tin box all the way to western Canada, that kettle should be filled with..."

Howard interrupted, "CAJUN GOLD!"

"No way," Les said, "Can't fool us again. We're not..."

"STUPID!" Norma Jean yelled.

"All right, Norma Jean," Dad said, "That's not necessary."

"But it's true," she whispered loud enough for the boys to hear her.

"Pull some of that out, Howard, and tell me what you think, Les," Dad said.

Howard did as he was told and turned to show the boys. "This is what Cajun gold looks like, boys. You almost lost our Acadian treasure."

The boys were silent, staring at the gold coins that were spilling out of Howard's hands.

Ralph whistled, "Good thing I'm here," he touched his police gun. "This is worth a lot of money!" He gazed around the empty hayfield and relaxed again.

The family was silent for some moments until...

Grrrrrrrrrr

It was Howard's stomach. Everyone laughed. Dad packed up the treasure box and the women went into the cabin to bring out the baked beans, potatoe salad, coleslaw, BBQ sauce, applesauce and plenty of cold pop. The pork was uncovered and the feast began, Grand-mère heading the line.

Norma Jean watched as Grand-père Leblanc took a plate of food and walked toward the knoll. He sat on the ground beside the great-great-grand-mère and stayed there for the rest of the evening.

Dixie did her best to sit beside any and all of the boys who in turn made it a game to stay away from her. Norma Jean watched them with both scorn and interest. No, she was not going to be like Dixie. Nor did she see any reason why she would want to sit beside her big stupid brothers.

But she did see why family mattered. It mattered a lot. What's past mattered. What's present mattered. And what's future mattered. Her biggest treasures were standing at the table, scooping up potatoe salad and asking for another serving of roasted pork.

Her thoughts were interrupted by Les: "What are we gonna do with that Cajun gold?" he asked.

The family grew quiet.

"A new boat?" Les continued.

"A new car!" Allan added.

"No, way," Keith scoffed. "A new TV!"

"You guys don't get it, do you?" Howard said above the din of laughter.

"What do you think, Howard?" Dad asked.

"It goes to the Dupre Museum, of course! It belongs in Nova Scotia in the museum that Gyp's parents are putting together right now."

Norma Jean looked at Howard. She wanted to say, *brilliant!* but she didn't. Instead, she smiled at him and then smiled at Gyp. That was enough.

"Wait a minute," Kathy said. "I thought this treasure was supposed to be handed down throughout the generations."

"Ya mean that gold belongs to me?" Allan said, stepping to the front of the peach pie line.

"No!" Norma Jean said, "At least not all of it." She looked at Mum. "Mum?"

Mum came up behind Grand-mère, hooked her arm and said, "That treasure box is going to get added to and taken away from, isn't it, Mère?"

"What do you mean?" Grand-mère asked.

"Well, your peach pie recipe is going to get added, and yes, some of the gold is going to go to the museum. AND a copy of the jambalaya recipe. But the Bible...that's ours. That belongs to our family and is never going to get lost again, is it, Allan?"

"Uh...,"Allan started nervously. "What do you want me to do with it?"

The family looked at each other, then Dad opened the treasure box lid. "It stays right here. Right where Bernard Richard Dupre left it."

"Yeah, but where does the treasure box go?" Norma Jean asked.

Again, the whole family looked at each other. The coondog howled and they looked over to where the Leblanc family had congregated, even Dixie. Ralph had gone back to active patrol duty after stuffing himself with pork and pie and it was just the family.

"I think the box stays on the shelf in the small cabin, amongst the books and dust. No one will bother it. After all, we didn't figure it out for years and truly, the clues were right under our noses," Norma Jean suggested.

Dad and Mum looked at each other, then at Grand-père and Grand-mère, who nodded.

"All right," Dad said. "Let's all take the box back where it belongs." He picked up the tin box and leading the family he walked down the lane, up the rickety porch steps, through the screen door and put the box on the shelf between *Aesop's Fables* and *The Jungle Book*.

Everyone cheered and Keith slapped Gyp on the back, sending him flying toward the closet. Gyp grabbed the heavy curtain which pulled off the nails and landed squarely on top of his head.

"Hey!" Keith called out. "Look!"

Gyp scrambled out from under the curtain and joined the rest of the family who were looking where Keith was pointing.

"What?" Norma Jean asked.

"It's a secret compartment!" Keith exclaimed. "Right there where the curtain was nailed!"

Norma Jean jumped into action, grabbed a kitchen chair and quickly put it next to the wall, reaching as high as she could to feel for an irregular wall board. "Where?!" she shouted, breathlessly. She looked back over her shoulder and saw the whole family watching her.

Suddenly, they all started laughing.

"Oh...you are...you are so..." Norma Jean was wordless. She fumed at Keith in silence as she took the chair back to the table.

The family slowly sauntered up the lane, back to the big cabin, ready to both clean up and go to bed. It had been a very, very, big day.

Later that night as the three kids were lying on their beds, moonlight slipping through every happy crevice of woodwork, they talked about having to say goodbye and when they could be together again. Norma Jean and Howard knew by now that Louisiana was a long, long way away. The chances of seeing Gyp again soon were narrow.

Norma Jean sighed as the conversation drifted into snores. She was going to miss this Cajun boy who had come with his chicory coffee and St. Afan prayers.

She got up from her bed, and sat down at the table, notebook in front of her. Clue Number 27: We've had a Gypsy Summer, and discovered that family is the greatest treasure.

Climbing back into bed, she let her gaze float through the cabin...the B.R.D. ghost...the stove pipe that was missing a key piece...the tin box that sat inconspicuously on the plankboard shelf...the closet wall that was missing a curtain...and the window frame that now had Gyp's initials carved in it.

What if there really WAS a secret compartment in the closet wall?

Once again she slipped out of bed, grabbed the notebook and quietly went out of the cabin to the porch. The moonlight shone its approval as she sat down on the steps and started writing...

Dear Diary,
Gyp is leaving tomorrow...

The End.

Fin.

Norma Jean and Howard's Notebook

CHAPTER 2

Clue Number 1: Our B.R.D ghost has a name and he's sleeping in the bed across the cabin: Bernard Richard Dupre.

Clue Number 2: The coondog and the great-great-grandmother from Spruce Bay are watching us and being really, really creepy.

Clue Number 3: OUR B.R.D. is involved in a mystery that involves a KEY.

Clue Number 4: Dixie's family is from Louisiana; Grand-père knows Gyp.

CHAPTER 3

Clue Number 5: What is *gris-gris*?

Clue Number 6: Great-great-grand-mère lives in a hut, hidden in the spruce grove.

CHAPTER 4

Clue Number 7: B.R.D. is mum's great-uncle; his nickname was Gypsy.

Clue Number 8:   Key—Gyp dreams about one;
                      Gyp's parents find one; Mum's
                      riddle has one. Why?

Clue Number 9:   *Gris-gris* means omens.

CHAPTER 5

Clue Number 10:   Gyp and Mum have the same
                      riddle.

Clue Number 11:   Nicky brings us a message.

CHAPTER 6

Clue Number 12:   Great-great-grand-mère's hut is
                      camouflaged by a nature-coded
                      backdoor and we found the
                      KEY.

CHAPTER 7

Clue Number 13:   Omens…more later.

CHAPTER 8

Clue Number 14:   Our families both have a
                      historical riddle that had
                      originally been given to *Marie*
                      from *Père*. They had been
                      stuffed into a 1730's French
                      Bible. It alludes to treasure.

What IS the treasure? Could it be Acadian gold?"

Clue Number 15:   The great-great-grand-mère sent us two omens: Hitchcock and the broomstick straws.

CHAPTER 9

Clue Number 16:   Mum gets a mysterious phone call from Grandad, and all of a sudden we're making a visit to them. She's worried about something.

Clue Number 17:   Great-great-grand-mère and Hitchcock are both giving us MOON omens.

CHAPTER 10

Clue Number 18:   The coondog visits our outhouse, bearing the same gift that Nicky had—the Acadian insignia.

Clue Number 19:   We follow the nature-lock and find the ruins of an old structure. The Acadian motto is inscribed into the cement.

CHAPTER 13

Clue Number 20:   Grandad confirmed that
                    B.R.D. and Gypsy somehow
                    hold the KEY to the lost family
                    treasure.

Clue Number 21:   My dear Marie,
                    You are the order to my pa<u>st</u>;
                    You are the j<u>oy</u> of my present;
                    You are the hope for my fu<u>tu</u>re.
                    The k<u>ey</u> to future happiness
                    is remembering your past.
                    If you do not, the key is not for
                    you, but for another.
                                Lo<u>ve</u>, Père
                    We solved the letters riddle:
                    S.T.O.V.E.

CHAPTER 14

Clue Number 22:   Granddad finds the key hidden
                    in the stove.

CHAPTER 15

Clue Number 23:   We think the treasure is hidden
                    in an Acadian foundation stone.

CHAPTER 16

Clue Number 24:   Treasure found; Treasure lost.

CHAPTER 17

Clue Number 25:   The Boys are STUPID.
Clue Number 26:   It's very satisfying to trick your older brothers.

CHAPTER 18

Clue Number 27:   We've had a Gypsy Summer, and discovered that family is the greatest treasure.

Norma Jean and the Mystery
of the Gypsy Summer

MYSTERY SOLVED

Howard Wayne and the Mystery of the Gypsy Summer

H.W. Nielsen

Chapter 1
A *FANTASTIQUE NIELSEN BOY*

"The lake was great. Pass the potatoes..." Howard said.

The End.

Fin.

About the Author:
Norma Jean's younger brother
Middle name: Wayne
Shoe size: 14.5

N.J. Bennett

About the Author:

N.J. Bennett grew up on a large grain farm, in a large family, and had an even larger imagination. Nature and all the abundance that it provides for creative play is a recurring theme in the Norma Jean Mystery series. Abandoned homesteads, tree forts, dugouts, grain fields, garbage dumps, ditches, haylofts, a turn-of-the-century farm home, a cabin at the lake, and a community school house, are all places a farm kid plays, and discovers mystery. As a first generation Canadian, the author is dedicated to writing and preserving a history of the family farm in the 1960's. Weaving farm life and Immigrant stories together into Middle Grade mysteries, N.J. Bennett teaches through story. Written into all the books is the use of a Clue Notebook into which the two protagonists, Norma Jean and Howard, write their observations as each mystery unfolds. Using words as math they cipher out the solution. Once a farm kid always a farm kid and N.J. Bennett is a farm kid. Married to Roy, (who at one point in his life lived in a teepee in the mountains) with two grown daughters, she now resides in Southern California, where she and her husband have made a fort in their backyard in which they sleep year-round.